Rite of Terror

Rose sat with the other members of the commune, deep within the mansion's huge underground room. The ritual was underway, and the room was filled with sweet-smelling smoke. She was experiencing a strange giddiness completely foreign to her, as she watched the weird spectacle on the stage.

The nearly nude girl assistants took a skeleton over to a guillotine and placed it on its knees with the skull head under the blade. Waring raised the guillotine's blade and it crashed down to sever the sack-covered skull from the body.

Next, a girl brought forward the skull in the black sack, as if to place it on the silver platter Waring held. But when she drew the sack away it revealed instead the gore-splattered head of the poet with whom Rose's missing friend, Helen, had run away —the head of Jules Bayliss!

Avon books by
Clarissa Ross

Clarissa Ross

A Hearse for Dark Harbor

AVON
PUBLISHERS OF BARD, CAMELOT, DISCUS, EQUINOX AND FLARE BOOKS

A HEARSE FOR DARK HARBOR is an original publication of Avon Books. This work has never before appeared in any form.

AVON BOOKS
A division of
The Hearst Corporation
959 Eighth Avenue
New York, New York 10019

ISBN: 0-380-00117-9

First Avon Printing, September, 1974.

AVON TRADEMARK REG. U.S. PAT. OFF. AND FOREIGN COUNTRIES, REGISTERED TRADEMARK—MARCA REGISTRADA, HECHO EN CHICAGO, U.S.A.

Printed in the U.S.A.

To Pat and Bob Neeley with memories of Kennebunkport, New York, and Boston!

Chapter One

Rose Marks suddenly became aware that Derek was driving toward Monastery Road, rather than to Dark Harbor and the ferry, where she'd expected to be taken. She gave the handsome, brown-haired young man a troubled look.

"We're heading in the wrong direction," she said.

Derek Mills glanced at her briefly, a sad smile playing about his lips. "I thought you might like to have a last look at the monastery. We have plenty of time."

"Oh!" she said in a knowing tone, and lapsed into silence as he drove on.

She gazed at the big houses along the road to the monastery and tried to remember which belonged to Derek. She'd been there mostly after dark, so it was hard to pick out the house.

She'd packed carefully for her return trip to New York via bus. Then she'd waited for Derek to come for her in his blue convertible. He'd insisted over her protests that he wanted to drive her to the ferry. She had a horror of good-byes and told him so, but he claimed that didn't matter. So she reluctantly agreed to let him come for her.

A summer romance! She supposed that was what many people on the island derisively termed it, but Rose felt it had been a good deal more than that. It was likely that Derek had saved her life and surely had prevented her from becoming involved with a dangerous and disreputable group.

She'd known from the beginning that he was married and that he loved his wife, Joyce, who was in a mainland hospital suffering from a second nervous breakdown. It was whispered around the island that this time she might not recover. It was a bleak prospect for Derek, who'd already battled through one breakdown of his wife's, following the loss of their only child under tragic circumstances.

Rose had not planned for she and the young member of the Dark Harbor Town Council to have a close friendship. It had simply happened—without either seeming able to do anything about it. Perhaps their mutual need for affection had been the key. She'd had no wish to steal Joyce's husband.

Although she had not met Joyce, she had seen her photo in the living room of the home on Monastery Road, which Derek had purchased for his ailing wife in the hope that it might help her regain her health. Unfortunately it hadn't. So Derek was living alone when Rose met him. Before long they knew that despite the barrier between them, they cared a great deal for each other.

Their friendship had caused gossip. Ugly rumors had spread quickly the length of the fourteen-mile-long island off the tip of Cape Cod. Pirate Island was no different from other isolated places in that the local community fully enjoyed any hint of scandal.

Knowing this, the romance between herself and Derek had been kept within carefully restricted bounds. They had both accepted the fact that it would end when she left the island. But the gossips made the worst of it.

Rose learned of the gossip she and Derek had inspired shortly before she'd made the decision to leave Pirate Island and return to her secretarial job in New York. When she found out what people were saying she was embarrassed and worried for Derek. He had assured her that the gossip didn't bother him in the least and that it would die down shortly. He'd added that any unpleasantness he might face because of it had been more than made up by their three-month friendship.

She hoped this was true, for the latest word was that Joyce could not be released in the foreseeable future. And Rose felt that by the time Derek's wife did return, the island busybodies would be wagging their tongues over somebody else's life.

She'd tried to hide her own heartbreak over saying good-bye to Derek, but now that he'd insisted on driving her to the ferry she worried about her ability to mask her feelings. She'd managed to maintain a façade of casualness thus far, but this unexpected detour to the monastery was more than a little upsetting.

The monastery had first brought her to Pirate Island—or at least her belief that she would find her missing friend, Helen, there. What this had led to still haunted her. That part of her experience on the island was an ugly dream which she tried to tell herself had never happened. Yet she knew that it had.

They drove past a three-story Victorian house which she was sure was Derek's place. The wind was blowing through her long black hair. She turned to him with an eager look on her face.

"That's your place we just passed, isn't it?" she asked.

Derek nodded. He was unusually solemn, she thought. "That's right," he said. "It's going to seem even bigger and lonelier from now on!"

"Derek!" Her throat constricted at his words.

"Sorry," he said. "That was stupid and cruel of me."

"As long as you know," she said, rebuking him.

Soon she was able to see the monastery, standing high on the cliffs ahead. She remembered how impressed she'd been when she'd heard its history. She'd lived in the monastery for a while without knowing the truth. Then after she had met Derek, who had written a history of the island, he told her of its origins. . . .

"More than a century ago," Derek said, "a ship was wrecked on the treacherous reefs at this end of the island. The sailors stayed on here and became fishermen and lived in the various villages on the island, including Dark Harbor. They built homes and quite a few of them married island girls. Then the doctor in Dark Harbor was suddenly confronted with a plague. Because he'd had some experience in Asia as a young man, it didn't take him too long to realize that there was an epidemic of leprosy among the islanders.

"At that time leprosy was a dread word. The cures of today were unknown and the disease caused a long and disfiguring illness ending in death. The leper was from Biblical times the symbol of the unclean. It did not take the doctor long to trace the disease to the shipwrecked sailors. Quite a few had been infected with the disease and spread it. The doctor at once isolated those stricken with leprosy from the healthy and moved them to the far end of the island, where they built shanties on the cliffs.

"This was in 1823 and no hospitals were on the island. A frantic call was sent out for medical and nursing aid. And in this case the appeal for help was answered by a religious order. A dedicated order of Roman Catholic monks offered to come to the island and build a monastery, combined with a hospital, to care for the lepers. Even though Pirate Island had been a Quaker stronghold from the earliest days of its development, the inhabitants welcomed the monks.

"The monastery proved a blessing for the islanders. The ravages of leprosy horribly mutilated the majority of those stricken with the disease. But in spite of their repulsive condition they lived on. The lepers had to be kept away from the healthy on the island and so the monastery and its grounds became their world. From time to time other patients with the disease arrived from the mainland for treatment there.

"Then about a half century ago leprosy was conquered to a great degree. Only rarely did the disease appear in the Western world. The patients of earlier days had died and the monks found themselves without lepers to care for. So the order sold the monastery to a wealthy man who converted it into a luxurious summer home while retaining its exterior. Unhappily, tragedy struck his family and he ended a suicide. Rumors that the place is haunted and cursed abound—and it well could be when you consider that Phillip Waring and his cult were the next to take it over. But you already know about that. . . ."

There had, indeed, been no need to tell her about that period of the monastery's history, for she had lived through it and knew about it only too well.

The car drew nearer the huge, gray, fortresslike structure with its top story redesigned as a lookout. The hippies who'd lived there under the leadership of Phillip Waring had called it the balcony and had often gone up there to sun themselves.

Derek parked the convertible in a flat field just below the monastery. Then they got out of the car and strolled together toward the cliff-edge. Derek claimed they would have plenty of time. They halted at the path that ran along the edge and stared at the monastery rising above them a short distance away.

"I suppose I'll always have nightmares about it," Rose said.

Derek, standing a few feet away from her with his hands in his pocket and his eyes squinted against the sun, nodded. "Probably."

"I didn't believe such things could happen to me," she said in awe as she studied the small windows of the former monastery. She'd occupied a tiny room on the third floor with a window that looked out on the ocean.

"I thought you might like a last look before we drove to the ferry," Derek said.

"I wouldn't have suggested it," she replied with a wry smile. "But now that I am here I can't say that I'm sorry. It may make it easier to forget later on; it seems so quiet now."

"There can't be more than a dozen in the place now," Derek informed her. "And I doubt if they can manage the upkeep and mortgage for long."

"Then what?"

"I don't know," he said, turning to her with a weary look on his handsome face. "I've had letters from the Holiday Inn people inquiring if it might be sold."

"Is that possible?"

"Perhaps. In the end they might decide to just use the location, tear the old building down, and begin all over again."

She frowned and said, "I don't know if I'd like that. It's been here so long and it does mean something in the history of the island."

"True."

"What is your personal opinion?"

"As a member of the Dark Harbor council, I am careful in expressing my opinions before a problem goes to vote."

Her smile was plaintive. "I won't be here to repeat your views."

"I'd almost forgotten," he said. "In that case, I'll be frank. I think Pirate Island could do with a Holiday Inn, but I'd just as soon see it located in the village of Dark Harbor, or anywhere but on the ground where the monastery stands."

"So you're against it."

"Yes. I think the monastery should be left. We could divide it up and make a paying condominium property of it while still retaining its outer character."

She nodded approval. "I like that idea."

He sighed. "Well, we'll see." And he glanced at the ancient structure once again.

Rose gave him a warm look. "I'm glad you've got the island and its problems. It keeps you busy."

He looked at her again. "Yes. And now I'm going to need that more than ever."

Her eyes met his. "You'll manage," she said softly.

"I wonder."

"I know."

He said, "I will hear from you, won't I?"

"Would that be wise?"

Derek seemed dismayed. "But I want to know about you. I have an interest in what happens in your life."

"And I have an interest in you," she said quietly.

"Then we must keep in touch."

"Perhaps."

"I want your promise!"

She looked at the ocean. "We'll see."

He came close to her and touched her arm. "I need something to hold onto. They're very pessimistic about Joyce. She may never be back."

Rose turned to him. "I'm so sorry."

"So am I," he said grimly. "Perhaps they're wrong. Time will tell, but meanwhile I go on living and hoping."

She said, "I think we should leave. I mustn't miss the ferry. It's the one the bus meets and I want to be in New York by tonight."

He studied her wearily. "We won't miss it," he promised, though he didn't budge. "When you're back in New York working again, will you remember Cape Cod and the island?"

"Of course."

"How long will you remember?"

"Pirate Island will always have a special meaning for me if only because of Helen," she said. "You know that."

"Yes, I guess I do," he agreed.

She gave him a pleading look. "Now we really should go!"

"Very well," he said, his voice husky. He stared at her a long moment and then very gently took her in his arms for a long kiss.

When he finally released her, he said, "That's the good-bye I won't be able to give you at the ferry wharf with all the gossips watching."

She nodded, her eyes sparkling with tears. "Yes. Won't they be disappointed when we say good-bye with a handshake?"

He laughed loudly and bitterly. "It will go a long way toward spoiling the autumn for them. They've gotten so much enjoyment talking about us all summer."

"They'll find someone else," she said.

"Never fear," he said as he led her by the hand back to the convertible.

As she walked with him her eyes fixed for a final moment on the monastery. A gull wheeled overhead, its loud harsh call knifing through her. And in that moment the monastery took on an even more somber tone. She saw it with different eyes. She was thinking of the nights of terror she'd known there. The fear and despair that had racked her as she witnessed pagan rites on the high balcony under the moonlight. And then there had been the unbelievable cruelty of the rituals in the torchlit cellar. Within those gray walls she had encountered violence and murder and a kind of life she'd never guessed existed.

At the car Derek gave her a worried look. "You're trembling," he said worriedly.
"Sorry," she said. "I was just remembering."
"The monastery?"
"Yes."
He looked haunted. "Try not to. Just remember it was that which brought you to me."
She smiled at him. "Yes. I can think of that and be grateful." She climbed into the car.
Derek closed her door and then went around and got in behind the wheel. She gave one last final glance over her shoulder at the old monastery standing out starkly against the sky as he drove away.
Then Rose turned around and stared straight ahead of her. "Maybe it should be torn down. Perhaps I'd feel better if it were."
Derek said nothing. They drove in silence for a while. Soon they came to the scattered houses lining the outskirts of the island's principal town, Dark Harbor. Then they entered Dark Harbor itself with its crooked streets and its main throughfare descending steeply down to the wharves. The cobblestones over which they drove had been used as ballast on the ships which thronged there in the great days of the whaling boom. The ramshackle buildings on either side of the street were all familiar to Rose. She saw the neon signs of Kimberly's Bar and Hotel and remembered the bad reputation the place had.
At last they reached the ferry wharf where the ferry waited to pull out. There was not as much traffic at this time of the year as in the peak tourist months, yet the wharf was filled with people and cars. Derek drove as near as he could. Then he helped her out of the car and went around to the trunk to get her bags.
She stood waiting for him when Dr. Henry Taylor stopped to talk to her. She knew the island's seventy-five-year-old doctor well. It was when she had consulted him that he suggested she talk to Derek about her problems.
The veteran doctor seemed mildly surprised. "Are you leaving us?" he asked.
She managed a wan smile. "Yes, time to go back to New York and my job."
His pleasant unlined face smiled in return. "I'd hoped

we'd won you over. That you were going to become an islander."

"I've been tempted," she said.

Dr. Taylor said, "Well, you can always come back. The ferry plies both ways, you know."

"I'll keep that in mind."

The old man eyed her seriously now. "You're feeling all right?"

"Yes."

"The nightmares don't bother you any more?"

"Only now and then."

He nodded gravely. "Maybe it will be better if you leave for a little. It's all too close behind you now. Later it won't be the same."

"I hope not," she said.

"I'm positive of it," the doctor assured her.

Derek came along with the bags and nodded to the old man. "She's leaving us, Henry."

"So she tells me," the doctor said. "Well, I have an idea that maybe it's just temporary."

"I wish you'd make her promise that," Derek said.

Rose smiled again. "I'll have to hurry. I think they are waiting only for me. Good-bye, Doctor."

The old man raised his soft hat and shook hands with her at the same time. His grip was strong and sincere. "Good-bye, Miss Marks. Good luck to you."

"Thank you," she said. "And to you!"

He chuckled. "The usual routine of mumps, measles, and arthritis, you know. Whoever said the life of a small-town doctor was exciting?"

"I shall always be grateful to you," Rose said.

She went on to buy her ticket while Derek saw that her luggage was taken aboard. Her ticket in hand, she went back to meet him.

They stood on the wharf, conscious that many of the islanders gathered there watched them. She gave him a direct look, "Good-bye again, Derek."

He took her hand. "Good-bye, Rose. I'll be waiting for those letters."

She nodded, too pained to answer, and not wanting to weep in public. She turned and hurried aboard the ferry. She waved to Derek as the ferry's engines throbbed and the vessel headed for the Cape Cod mainland. Derek waved back as the distance between wharf and ferryboat widened.

Rose ignored her fellow passengers and leaned on the iron railing and stared out across the water. As Dr. Taylor had said, the ferry plied both ways and it did not seem all that long ago that she'd been aboard it for the first time on her way to Pirate Island with all the strange experiences she was to undergo still before her. It seemed an age ago—and yet it was only a matter of a few months. Her mind went back to the beginning. It had all started the night she and her roommate, Helen Grant, had gone together to the cocktail party in the Village. It had been one of those noisy, crowded affairs which she almost immediately regretted attending. Probably a hundred people crowded into the small apartment. The heat, smoke, and noise were like an endurance test.

The bar was in the kitchen and drinks were hard to get. She and Helen had met only two or three people whom they knew and after a half hour of standing together in bedlam, they decided to go home rather than brave the kitchen for a second drink.

Helen, a pert blonde with a heart-shaped face, sighed. "I don't think we'll miss anything or be missed if we leave!"

Rose replied, into her friend's ear, "I decided that five minutes ago."

"Let's find a place for these empty glasses and then make an exit," Helen said, and she turned and pushed her way through the softly lighted living room. Rose followed.

They had not gone more than a few feet when their way was blocked by a tall, red-haired youth wearing a black turtleneck and blue jeans. He had a bronze medallion hanging from a chain around his neck and down his sweater front and his bright-red hair framed his long, narrow face. He smiled at them, exuding a kind of decadent charm.

"Darlings! You're not leaving so soon!" he exclaimed, reprimanding them.

"Too crowded!" Helen said.

"That's it," Rose agreed.

"People are most interesting in crowds," he informed

them. His hair reached to his shoulders. "Let me have your glasses and the name of your favorite brew and I shall tilt with the bartenders for your delight!"

They asked him for vodka and water and he vanished at once, shoving his way through the crowds with some special technique which had a good deal to do with his thin stature and tallness.

Helen watched him go with an expression of amused dismay on her pretty face. "What do you make of that?" she asked loudly.

"He's interesting but far-out! But then so are most of the guests!" Rose replied in an equally loud voice. It didn't matter; everyone was screaming at everyone else and no one could be heard much less overheard.

Rose and Helen were both private secretaries with the same large industrial firm uptown. They had met at work and discovered that both were alone in the city. Helen at once had suggested they share an apartment, and it had turned out successfully.

They were of contrasting physical appearance and temperament. Rose was dark, serious, and quiet while blonde Helen was fun-loving and outgoing. Helen's impulsive nature often got them into predicaments, the cocktail party being a typical example.

In a surprisingly short time the tall, red-haired young man pushed his way back to them with their drinks held high above the heads of the crowd.

Reaching them, he presented them with the vodkas and announced, "My name is Jules Bayliss! I'm a poet!"

Helen stared at him and Rose worried that the brash young man might hurt Helen, who was all too easily swept away by first impressions. And right now she had a gleam in her large gray eyes. Helen at once introduced them to the young man and then asked, "What poetry have you written? I've never heard of you!"

The lean-faced man recited: "Music resembles poetry; in each are nameless graces, which no methods teach. And which a master hand alone can read!"

Helen's face brightened. "That's very good!"

Rose spoke up quickly. "It should be! Alexander Pope wrote it two centuries ago!"

The tall young man showed a quick moment of shock

and then he hastily regained his composure and gave Rose one of his easy smiles. "You are absolutely correct! That was a little joke on my part. I was going to cue you in at once, but you beat me to it."

Helen asked him, "What have you written?"

" 'Canto To Washington Square,' " he replied at once. "It's too long to quote from here. I read it in a half dozen of the coffee houses and they loved it!"

"Has it been published?" Rose asked. She was beginning to feel the glib young man was a faker and that Helen had taken too great a liking to him. She now desperately wanted to discredit him if she could.

He shook his head and in an arrogant, bored voice said, "Who wants to publish nowadays? And where is the medium?" He went on talking in this fashion and Rose became increasingly wary of him. At this point, the host of the party arrived and hurried her away to meet some other guests. She lost contact with Helen and the supposed poet. When she was free again she couldn't find them. They had left the party together without telling her.

Rose was upset. She had never known Helen to do anything like this. She was faced with riding the subway alone and a walk of several long blocks to the apartment. She hoped that Helen and the thin young man might already be there, but they weren't.

It was midnight before Helen arrived home. Rose was at once aware of the dreamy look on her friend's face and shocked by the ecstatic manner in which the blonde girl spoke about Jules Bayliss.

"We strolled up Fifth Avenue and he told me all about where he lives. It's on an island, a place off Cape Cod known as Pirate Island."

"I've heard of it," Rose said. "It's mainly a summer resort. There's a town called Dark Harbor where the ferry puts in."

"That's right," her friend said enthusiastically as they sat together in the tiny kitchen of their apartment over midnight coffee. "Jules is a member of a commune there. He says it's a wonderful group. Their leader is a kind of mystic by the name of Phillip Waring."

Rose frowned. "From what I've heard of those communal groups I wouldn't be impressed. In fact I don't much care for Jules. I'm sure he was ready to lie about his poetry and I think he'd be a poor person to depend on."

Helen looked hurt. "I think you're jumping to conclusions. He's really very nice. Of course he's poor and unrecognized, but he could turn out to be a successful poet."

"I'd like to read some of his work before deciding that."

"He said he'd bring some of his things around," Helen said. "Guess where the commune has its headquarters? In a monastery where lepers used to be treated! He says the atmosphere there is wonderful and they have a great group of young people. It's the only place he can write his poetry."

"I hope he's going back soon."

"In a week or two. I've invited him here for dinner tomorrow night. I do hope you'll try and like him."

"I won't make any promises yet," Rose said cautiously.

Later she was glad that she hadn't. Jules Bayliss arrived the next night wearing the same shabby outfit he had worn at the party. He had not shaved and he mumbled some excuses about having been to a pot party and not getting away when he'd expected. His whole manner was wild and disjointed and Rose found herself even more critical of him than before.

At dinner, he boasted, "I'm a Satanist! Everyone at the monastery is. Phillip has the whole thing worked out—you ought to hear his philosophy!"

Rose gave the thin, red-haired youth a scornful glance. "Your Phillip Waring sounds like a New England Charles Manson!"

He smiled cynically. "You don't like me, do you?"

"I think not," she said carefully.

An embarrassed Helen said, "Rose likes to say outrageous things! Don't mind her!"

"I don't," Jules replied, a nasty gleam in his eye. "But I can't see how you can develop into any kind of a real person with someone like her dominating you."

Helen blushed in embarrassment. "You're wrong. Rose doesn't try to dominate me!"

"It seems like it to me," the poet said.

Rose snapped back at him with: "Do you think she'd be under less domination in a Satanist commune?"

Helen pleaded, "Rose!"

Following the meal, Rose excused herself and went out to a movie. When she returned, Jules had gone and Helen was curled up in bed waiting for her.

As soon as Rose came into the room, Helen said cheerfully, "I had a grand evening. You should have heard Jules's poetry."

"I'll bet," she'd replied dryly.

Helen sat up. "Honestly, it was good. He left early because he had to meet some friends in the Village. He's going back to Pirate Island in a few days."

"Good!"

"I'll miss him!" Helen said protestingly. "He's so exciting!"

"You hardly know him!"

"I feel I know him better than most men I've met," her pretty blonde girlfriend said. "And you know what?"

"What?"

"He's offered to get me a place in the commune if I go back to the island with him!" Helen's face was ecstatic.

Rose sank unhappily onto the bed. "You're joking!"

"Oh, I haven't thought seriously about it."

"I should hope not!"

"But I am going to miss him!" Helen said, sighing.

Rose should have interpreted this as a storm warning and been prepared for what was to follow soon after. But when she arrived home after work a week later to find an apologetic note on the kitchen table with half a month's rent money beside it, she was completely shocked.

Helen had run off to Pirate Island with Jules Bayliss! In the note she explained that she'd gotten a leave of absence from her job and planned to remain on the island for a trial period. She apologized for leaving Rose with the burden of paying the full apartment rent and promised she'd return there again if she came back. At the moment she felt her future lay with Jules at the commune.

Helen had cleared all her things out of the apartment. There were almost no traces of her left. Rose checked with the office and found her friend had terminated her association with the company. There had been no leave of absence.

Rose felt deceived, but did not want to desert Helen at a time when Rose felt she might be needed. So Rose wrote her and hoped the letter would be delivered. A reply came from Helen in which she stated how happy she was and that she never wanted to return to New York.

Rose still did not give up. She wrote Helen that she would retain the apartment alone in hopes that Helen might change her mind and return. Helen thanked Rose in a second reply letter, but saw little possibility of herself ever leaving the commune.

The more Rose remembered Jules Bayliss the more sinister he became. She found herself continually anxious about Helen's welfare and tried to think of some ways in which she might help her. She consulted friends in Greenwich Village whom she felt might know something more about the island commune.

A bearded hippie in a tiny shop that sold way-out men's clothing was pessimistic. "They're a tough outfit! Jules was on heroin a few years ago. And some say that's why Phillip Waring founded the commune. It's a hideaway for drug addicts."

Her eyes opened wide in fear. "Do you think that may be true?"

"It could be exaggerated," he admitted. "A lot of the stories you hear are. But I do know Jules was on dope. Your girlfriend has found herself some bad friends."

"I'm sure of it," she replied, sighing. "But you can't convince her!"

"I guess the main thing would be to keep in touch with her," the hippie said. "If you can catch her at a point when she becomes disillusioned, maybe you can get her away from there."

"I'll keep writing." Rose said determinedly. And she did.

But Helen's letters became less frequent as the weeks went by. Then for a long while there was no letter from Helen at all. Then Rose received a very strange letter in which Helen begged her not to write again or try and get in touch with her.

Rose read the letter with a feeling of impending disaster. And the face of the arrogant Jules Bayliss shone in her memory, more hateful than ever. Rose made an appointment at once with a lawyer who knew Helen.

When she was shown into the lawyer's office she said confidingly, "I don't know what to do!"

The lawyer looked grave. "I've been wondering how much you knew about all this."

"I knew she left her job and moved there with this Jules Bayliss."

"Did you also know that she recently drew all her money from her savings account and had it sent to Dark Harbor?"

Rose was aghast. "She drew all her money out?"

"All of it," the lawyer said. "And for a girl of Helen's age it was quite an amount."

"They're bleeding her of every penny!" she gasped. "And when it's gone what will happen?"

"If I know men of that caliber he'll likely pick some fight with the idea of her leaving or giving him an excuse to ask her to leave!"

"Poor Helen!"

"It's too bad. She has an uncle living in Utah and that's about all."

Rose looked at him anxiously. "Have you written him?"

"Yes, I decided I should write," the lawyer said. "Her uncle didn't seem worried about her. She'd made up a story for him of her marrying and going to Europe."

"And she's done neither."

"No."

"I didn't like that young man. And now this letter from her asking me not to write to her again—it isn't Helen!"

"I'm entirely in agreement with you on that," the lawyer said.

Rose sighed. "I'm afraid for her!"

"You should be," the lawyer said sadly.

Chapter Two

Rose wrote to Helen several more times, but her letters were returned. Feeling miserable and hurt, Rose could not decide what to do. Had Helen found such a satisfying life with Jules Bayliss that she didn't need any of her old friends? Or had she been swallowed up by the sinister group on the island?

Then she had the nightmare. One night in late April there was an unusual heat wave and the apartment became unbearable. She opened the windows and turned off all the radiators, but it did little good. And when she finally went to bed she twisted and turned for a long while.

When sleep came at last it brought a hideous nightmare. She dreamt that she was in a gray room. In one corner stood an open gray casket mounted upon silver supports. As she neared the casket, she saw Helen in it—Helen, with the waxen face and closed eyes of the dead, dressed in gray to match the casket and the room.

Rose let out a piteous cry of sorrow and despair as she stared into the coffin. Then she heard a rustle in the shadowy corner behind the coffin and saw a thin figure wearing a gray robe. Jules Bayliss!

"Now she is truly one of us!" the ghostly figure of Jules intoned. "A daughter of the night! She has come to Satan!"

"Murderer!" Rose screamed, across the casket of her friend.

He laughed softly. She screamed again and was still screaming when she awoke. She stared into the warm darkness and knew that she had to find out about her friend. She could not go on without discovering what had really happened to Helen.

The next day she asked for a leave of absence, which was granted. She found the bus would be the least expensive and most direct route to the ferry. She kept her luggage as light as possible, since there would be several transfers along the way. She took several hundred dollars from her savings account with her and arranged to draw further on her account, if necessary, through the bank at Dark Harbor. Now that she was doing something positive about finding her friend some of her tension left her, but she still worried a great deal about Helen.

On a pleasant day in early May she started on her journey. After the long bus trip, she embarked on the ferry. Aside from the usual natives and vacationers, there was one unusual character, a large young man with long black hair wearing a cowboy outfit. His suede jacket was trimmed with fringe and a staggering variety of beads, but what made him the center of attention was the hearse he drove. It wasn't just a hearse, but it was an ancient hearse, probably about thirty years old.

It was black with glass sides and the car body on which it rested was three decades out of style. But the hearse was in good condition and the big hippie had polished it so that it shone.

When she saw the big young man leaning at the ferry's rail next to the hearse, she felt that luck was on her side at last. Judging by the looks of the young man he had to be on his way to the hippie commune; he might know something about Jules Bayliss and Helen.

With a brashness foreign to her she went over to him and said, "Hello! May I ask you something?"

The big, dark-haired youth had a round, good-natured face. He grinned at her lazily. "You sure as heck can! My name is Tex. What's yours?"

"I'm Rose," she replied, and then decided it would be best to use a name other than her own until she was certain about him. "Rose Smith!"

His black eyes mocked her. "Smith! Now that's a real unusual name!"

"I like it. I'm used to it."

"Good," he said, continuing in the same joking way. "Will you tell me what it was you wanted to ask me?"

The huge, black-haired young man was no fool despite his outfit and the ancient hearse he drove. Very carefully, she began, "I'm entranced by your mode of transportation."

"Can't recommend it for a final jaunt," he told her. "Otherwise it's okay! But that can't be what you wanted to ask me."

"No," she said. "It wasn't. I'm interested in where you're going."

She saw him become visibly guarded in manner. His eyes fixed on her. "You are?"

"Yes," she said, forcing herself to seem friendly and casual. "I'll bet you're headed for the old monastery!"

"Old monastery?"

"You know where I mean," she insisted. "You're just playing dumb. It's on the island! The monastery where the lepers used to be."

He towered above her, still none too friendly. "What do you know about the monastery?"

She smiled. "I know that Phillip Waring has his commune there and you're probably part of it. I bet you're taking that hearse to him."

"You're quite a one for putting things together," Tex said, still rather hostile. "How do you know about Phillip Waring?"

"I met somebody who told me about his commune."

The big man looked at her and then slapped his thigh and guffawed. "Now that beats all! You don't expect me to believe that! Why you even wear shoes! What friend of yours would know about us?"

"A girl I met at a cocktail party," she said, careful not to name names or suggest it was anyone she knew well.

"There's a lot of silly talk goes on at cocktail parties. You can't depend on what you hear."

"Phillip Waring still is living at the monastery with his followers, isn't he?"

"You're not one of those newspaper reporters, are you?" the youth asked warily.

"No. My only interest is visiting the commune and maybe joining it."

His eyes widened. "Joining it?"

"Why not?"

"You're not the type!"

"From what my friend said you don't have to be any special type. But you do have to be accepted."

The black-haired Tex was skeptical. "You haven't any idea of what that means."

"Maybe not, but I'd like to find out. I want to go see Phillip Waring at the monastery. Will you take me there?"

Tex eyed her as he considered this. "I've got an idea Phil wouldn't thank me and maybe you wouldn't either."

"That's nonsense!" she protested.

"You really want to go there?"

"Would I ask you if I didn't?"

Tex shrugged. "All right. You can come along. But you'll be wasting your time. You're too square for the monastery."

She gave him an enigmatic smile. "Suppose we find that out after I get there."

Tex showed his first sign of friendliness. He grinned. "Well, if that is the way you want it!"

"Thanks. When we get off the ferryboat I can transfer my things to the hearse."

"Sure," Tex said, giving the ancient black vehicle an admiring glance. "A beauty, isn't she?"

"I can't imagine why anyone would want to part with her," Rose said in mock agreement. Actually she thought the hearse a somber, horrible-looking thing and imagined its owners must have been delighted to rid themselves of it.

"I got it for a song. Phil is going to be pleased. We

need extra transportation at the monastery and you can put a slew of people in this."

"You're thinking of a vertical position not a horizontal one."

He chuckled. "You're right."

They remained at the railing near the hearse, not paying any attention to the excitement the ancient vehicle caused among the others on board.

"You have a job?" Tex asked her.

"I did have."

"Now you want to try something else?"

"I think so."

"You have a boyfriend?"

"Not just now!"

He grinned again. "Have a fight with him?"

She didn't want to give him too much information, so she said, "Something like that."

"You can join my family if you stay," Tex told her.

"Oh?" It was her turn to raise eyebrows.

"Sure. I got me a couple of wives and some kids."

"Is that legal on Pirate Island?"

He shrugged and grinned. "As legal as it is anywhere. Phil sort of splits the group up in families. I head one of them."

Rose realized the situation could get pretty difficult, but she was still determined to search for Helen. "I suppose you get a lot of transients—people who come and go?"

"Some. Phil don't put up with deadheads long. He likes people to pay their share."

This at once interested Rose. "How is that done?"

"We expect the family to turn over whatever they have in cash to Phil. And if he finds anyone holding out it's too bad for them."

"Oh?" This had an ominous ring. And it explained why Helen had so abruptly drawn her savings out of the bank. Leader Phil Waring had probably used some force to get the money from her. And she could picture Jules Bayliss as a willing accomplice.

Tex gazed directly at her. "So you know what to expect."

She turned from him and stared out at the ocean, not

wanting him to notice her uneasiness. "Did you ever meet a blonde girl named Helen at the monastery?"

"Helen?"

"Yes."

The big man hesitated. "I don't think so."

She gave him a quick glance. "You don't remember?"

Tex's good-natured big face wore a cautious look. "I've been away a lot, sometimes for two and three weeks at a time. People come and go at the monastery. I could have missed this Helen. What was her last name?"

Again Rose felt she had to be on the alert, to pretend not to have known Helen too well. "I'm not sure of her last name. We just met casually, but she talked about the monastery. She'd either been here once or was coming here."

The black-haired man in the cowboy outfit smirked. "You can ask Phil when you see him."

"I will. Is the monastery a spooky place?"

Tex laughed. "Some of them think so."

"Do the ghosts of the monks or the lepers they used to care for come back and haunt the place?"

"There are stories," he admitted.

"What kind of stories?"

"Some claim to have seen the ghost of Leper Mary."

"Who was she?"

"According to the story she was the prettiest girl on the island two hundred years ago. She married one of those sailors with the leprosy and caught it from him. They were both put in the monastery to be cared for by the monks. And after a while her whole face rotted away and one stormy night she left her room and went up to the tower and jumped off. They found her dead on the rocks the next morning."

Rose shuddered. "What a tragic story!"

"Yeah," the big man said grimly. "According to those who claim to have seen the ghost, she wears a kind of veil over her head and a long black habit like a nun. And sometimes she stands before you and lifts the veil and you see that she has no face."

Rose stared at him. "Do you know anyone who has told you seriously that they've seen the ghost?"

He nodded. "One of my wives. Dallas. She's from down

our way, too. She says she's seen the ghost a couple of times. You can ask her."

"I'm not sure I want to," Rose said. The account of the ghost had frightened her.

"They tell those kind of stories about all old places. I don't put any stock in them."

"You're probably wise."

He turned and stared to the left. "Look," he said, "that's the island coming into view now. You can just see the shore."

And she gazed out across the silver of the sun-flecked ocean and saw that she could see the first faint shadow of Pirate Island on the water. As the ferry pushed its way nearer the island, Tex pointed out various landmarks. Bald Mountain, the highest spot on the island. Gull's Head light. He even indicated the tall cliffs where the monastery was located.

The ferry approached the Dark Harbor wharf and she had her first close glimpse of the town. Its hilly, cobblestoned main street stretched up from the docks and was lined with shabby one- and two-story structures. A host of fishing and pleasure craft were anchored in the harbor and the wharf bustled with activity.

She stood with Tex and studied the many parked cars and the people waiting for the arrival of the ferry. She said, "I had no idea there would be so many down to meet the boat."

"Ferry time is the big event on the island," Tex told her. "They come down whenever one comes in. And now the tourist season is near and the number of people here grows every day."

"I suppose so. And then in the fall again the population of the island decreases."

"Just the regulars," Tex agreed. "And Phil and some of us wintered here last year. There isn't any central heat at the monastery, but we managed somehow."

She didn't have time to question him about this, for the ferryboat docked and she had to look after her luggage. She worried that he might drive away without waiting for her, but he didn't. When she brought her bags to him he was still on the dock with the back doors of the hearse open.

He tossed her bags in the rear and invited her to get in the front seat with him.

All this time the odd vehicle was drawing marked attention from the bystanders. As they drove off, she heard one of the elderly fisherman say to another, "What will that bunch at the monastery think of next?"

She smiled at Tex as he drove the hearse slowly up the main street. "Your hearse attracted some humorous comments."

"We're used to that," he said cheerfully. "The island crowd get upset about anything that's different. They gave the real-estate man who let Phil have a lease on the monastery a lot of trouble. They didn't really want us on the island."

Rose could easily understand this, though she dared not voice her views to Tex. She was already feeling a little on edge, wondering how she'd manage when she reached the monastery. The way in which Helen had vanished served as a grim reminder of what might happen to her. At least she was going into this with her eyes open.

She asked, "You think the islanders would like to get rid of your commune?"

"They've been frank about that. They hear all kinds of talk about orgies and drugs and they think it's a rough place we're running."

"Is it?"

"Depends on your point of view," Tex told her as he wheeled the hearse off the main street and onto a highway.

"That could mean anything."

"We get all sorts. Phil isn't too strict about some things."

They drove along a road which ran near the water. Every so often they passed an estate and the view of the shore was beautiful.

Rose said, "The island has lovely scenery."

"Yes. We were lucky to get the monastery. They'd use any excuse they could find to get it back from us."

"Is that liable to happen?"

"Only if we can't keep up our payments," Tex said. "And Phil sees to that."

"He must be a good manager."

"He is," Tex said.

They reached an unpaved section of the road and the hearse bumped along on its rough surface, raising a cloud of dust.

Suddenly Tex said, "There you are! That's the monastery ahead."

She studied it and was at once struck by its stark, gray lines. It had the appearance of a fortress with its tiny windows and a tower with ramparts at the top level. Its gray, plain appearance at once struck a chord in her memory and she recalled that gray nightmare which had driven her to the island in search of Helen. In it she had seen her friend in a gray coffin. And the fact that the monastery was of the same color made her wonder if there mightn't have been some truth to her nightmare.

Tex drove the hearse straight up to the monastery and in through an arched entrance which led to a kind of walled courtyard. In the courtyard lolled a dozen or so hippies. They were all wearing clothes as bizarre as Tex's and both men and women had long hair and an unwashed look. They all converged around the hearse.

Tex got out and spoke to a few of them. Then he joined her and said, "I'll take you in to see Phil after I've talked to him myself. Your stuff will be safe in the hearse until you know what you want to do."

"All right," she said, feeling terribly out of it in her print summer dress with its neat white collar and cuffs.

Tex reached out and caught a tall, bony girl with a pert, freckled face and corn-silk straight hair hanging to her shoulders. He drew her to him and introduced her. "This is Dallas. You two can get to know one another." And to Dallas, he said, "Rose here thinks she wants to join us." He grinned at Rose and left them, walking up the steps that led to the cathedral-type entrance of the monastery.

Dallas gave her an appraising look with blue eyes too old and hard for her age. "Where did he pick you up?" she drawled.

Rose blushed. "He didn't. I came here on my own."

"You have to be joking," Dallas said. And Rose could now tell that the girl was even younger than she had seemed at first. Probably only in her late teens.

"I thought I'd like it here."

Dallas eyed her with derision. "In that outfit? Take a look around."

She managed a smile. "I've been traveling. I have other things to wear. And isn't it mainly what I think and feel and not what I wear that's important? I want to be a member of the commune."

The tall girl studied her suspiciously. "Why?"

"I have my own reasons."

"You expect to be one of Tex's wives? Then you better have plenty of cash. He's starving the ones he's got and the kids as well."

She knew her cheeks were red again. "I don't want to be in Tex's harem!"

Dallas laughed coldly. "If he wants it that way you will be or you'll move on."

"What makes you so sure of that?"

Dallas glanced sullenly toward the monastery. "Phil agrees to most everything Tex suggests. Phil depends on Tex."

The other hippies, having examined the hearse and gotten a good look at Rose, had wandered off to do their own thing again. They sprawled on the sunny spots of the courtyard. On the front steps a thin, youngish man with a head bald except for a rim of red hair and with a sparse red beard sat, nodding strangely every so often.

Rose asked Dallas. "Who is he?"

The tall, freckled girl in the shabby granny dress gave the man on the steps a disgusted look. "That's Cal! He's from 'Frisco and he's a nothing!"

"Just a kind of tramp?"

Dallas smiled sarcastically. "He hangs around because every so often he gets stuff from Phil. He's high now. Can't you tell?"

Rose stared at the emaciated man in dismay. "You mean he's a drug addict?"

"What else? Phil uses him. He can tell him to go into Dark Harbor and hoist anything and he comes back with it. There are stores and fine homes around the harbor and Cal does all right."

She looked up into the scornful face of Dallas. "He steals for his habit and Phil gives him heroin in exchange for the stolen goods?"

Dallas smiled coldly. "Don't say that I said it—you ought to be able to figure it out for yourself."

She could, but didn't want to. Her friend in the Village had been right. The commune fronted for all kinds of crime and was a haven for drug addicts. Jules Bayliss was one. What had he done to Helen?

"Do people stay here long?" she asked Dallas.

"Depends."

"On what?"

Dallas shrugged. "On how useful they are to Phil and on how much money they have."

"Money counts then?"

"Sure," the girl from Texas said derisively. "We get a lot of rich kids here!"

"Why?"

"They like the life and a lot of them are on pot and other stuff," Dallas said. "They know they can get it here."

"I see," Rose said.

Dallas took a look at the hearse and disgust showed on her tiny, freckled face. She had a small face for a girl her size. She said, "What would he bring back a thing like that for?"

"It was cheap."

"I can't think of any other reason!"

"He said that you needed transportation here."

Dallas said, "I'd just as soon die as ride in that." Then a smile of self-revelation spread across her freckled face and she added, "I guess if I died it wouldn't matter!" She laughed.

Rose smiled. "It caused a lot of comment at the wharf."

"I'll bet," the tall girl said sarcastically. "Likely they'll be after us to get out of here again. They've tried once."

"So I heard."

Dallas gave her an interested look. "Maybe if you want to stay here, and don't expect to be Tex's number-one wife, it would be okay. I'm his number-one wife."

"Thanks," Rose said quietly, "I'll remember that."

Tex lumbered out of the monastery and headed directly toward her. Reaching her, he said, "Phil will see you now."

"What about my things?" She indicated the hearse.

"I'll have Dallas take them inside and watch them until you've finished with Phil."

"All right."

The big, black-haired youth gave Dallas some instructions about the luggage, and then he escorted Rose inside. They walked down the middle of a big room, which must have been a chapel in the old days. It had later been converted into a large center drawing room with rich, walnut-paneled walls. Now it was almost devoid of furniture and the walls were bare of any kind of decoration as was the fireplace.

There was a door to the left and Tex led her through it to a stairway that led down. After a moment she found herself in a room that was actually a cellar, but seemed to have been cut out of the cliff. She judged that it must be located between the monastery and the edge of the cliff, since it had a single broad window looking out over the ocean. The window had a multi-paned frame and bowed outward. It gave the room plenty of brightness.

A dais stood by the window and seated at a desk on the dais was one of the most remarkable-looking people she'd ever seen. He was dark-haired and thin to the point of emaciation, his eyes large and bright, and on his thin face was a taunting smile. The thing that made him exceptional was the powerful personality one felt belonged to this thin young man.

Motioning to her to come closer, he said in a dry voice, "Well?"

Reluctantly she moved toward him, aware of the sharp, piercing eyes boring into her, thinking of the cruelty they suggested, and worrying about what might have become of Helen.

"You haven't answered me."

In a weak voice, she replied, "What am I to say?"

The emaciated face, with the flat, slanting forehead receding to thin black hair combed straight back and falling over his collar in the rear, showed grim distaste.

"Tex tells me you'd like to join us here."

"Yes," she replied weakly.

He shook his head. "I've never seen a more unlikely recruit. Did you see the crowd in the courtyard when you came in?"

"Yes."
"Notice any difference between them and you?"
"They are dirtier."
He seemed startled. Then he regained his poise. She saw that he wore slacks, a white shirt open at the neck, and a chain astrology plaque over his shirt.
He fingered the plaque as he smiled bleakly at her. "You surprise me. You have a sense of humor."
Quietly, she said, "I'm sure I would fit in here better than you think. A friend advised me that I would."
"What friend?"
She watched him closely. "Her name was Helen. I don't know her other name. We only met once and she said she was coming here."
He betrayed no hint of having heard the name before. "Is that why you are here?"
"Yes. She sent me one letter and told me how much she was enjoying herself here. That she'd found someone she loved and was never returning to New York. I'd given her my name and address, but she'd neglected to give me hers. She just signed her name, Helen, and I didn't have her last name."
"So?"
"I wrote a letter in reply here addressed to Helen, but it was returned to me. I wasn't able to get in touch with her. I waited for a while and no other letters came for me. So I decided to come here and find her myself."
Phil Waring's pale, emaciated face was stern as he crouched over the desk. "There is no Helen here."
"But there must have been for at least a little while!" she protested.
"I know of none. Why does she mean so much to you? You claim not to know her name, yet you've come hundreds of miles to find her!"
"Not to find her, really, but to find this place. She wrote me so glowingly of it I wanted to come here."
The leader of the commune frowned. "Tex says you told him you're not a reporter."
"No!"
"Nor a private investigator?"
"No, I'm not," she protested again.
His pale face wore an evil smile. "I hope you're telling

the truth. Dallas and Tex are going through your bags now. If they find anything to prove that you are you may be in trouble."

She gasped at the audacity of this calm revelation. And she was thankful she'd been careful not to include anything which might incriminate her in any way. She'd not even brought Helen's letters, which she'd pretty well memorized in any case. Her money was in a money belt that she was wearing at this moment and so they wouldn't get that.

"How dare they do that?"

The leader of the commune stood up. "Because I ordered them to do it."

"You did?"

He nodded. He was stooped for a young man and dreadfully thin. "You have come here to me and asked to be one of my group—have you a right to complain about anything I decide to do?"

She hesitated. "I suppose not. But I haven't been accepted by you, so you are taking in advance rights which aren't yours."

Phil Waring smiled nastily. "It is part of the indoctrination. What about money?"

"What about it?"

"Is it in your bags? Better tell me. Tex is apt to deny it and keep it for himself. I need to be able to deal with him."

She said carefully, "There is no money in the bags."

He frowned. "But you have money?"

"Yes. On my person."

"How much?"

She decided to tell him half of what she really had. "About a hundred and fifty dollars."

"Is that all?" he asked disgustedly.

"I can get more. I had my bank transfer money to an account in the Dark Harbor bank."

The emaciated face showed renewed interest. "Indeed. Then you felt that you would be accepted here?"

"I hoped so. I want the freedom living here will offer me. And I think my friend Helen might return here. I'm very anxious to meet her again."

The leader of the commune fixed his luminous black

eyes on her. "You will have no freedom here, other than that I decide to allow you. And your friend Helen obviously lied to you. She was never here."

"She wrote me from here!"

"She must have pretended she was writing from the monastery," he said. "She could have been merely a visitor on the island."

Rose knew this was not so. Helen had definitely written her of her experiences at the monastery and of Jules Bayliss being there. For some reason it was impossible for her to understand, the leader of the commune was denying any knowledge of Helen. There was the question of Helen's money, but surely the commune crowd could have gotten that and then turned Helen out. Instead she'd simply vanished.

"I have a feeling she will turn up," Rose insisted stubbornly.

The thin young man curled his lip at this. "And you expect to be allowed to stay here?"

"I believe in what you have to offer."

"Do you?" he inquired sarcastically. "Then suppose I assign you to Tex's family to be his fourth wife."

"I'm willing to be a member of Tex's family," Rose said. "I'm not interested in being his fourth or any other wife."

"You disobey me already? That is a poor start."

"There are some orders I can't accept from you. That is one of them. But I will pay well to be allowed to remain here. And when the cash I have is used up I'll get more from the bank in Dark Harbor."

The stooped man's emaciated face took on a crafty look. "It will cost you a hundred a week."

"Very well."

"And no complaints."

"All I ask is a room, a minimum supply of food, and a chance to study your rituals and your way of life."

He took on an air of importance. "We have the new path to the ultimate in happiness," he informed her. "You can learn a great deal here. I have solved the secret of pain. Let me show you!"

He went to the desk and opened a drawer. From it he drew out a giant needle, which he held up for her to see.

Then in the manner of a sideshow fakir he plunged it through the back of his hand so that the point showed through his palm. Coming close to her he held out the palm and brought the point of the needle up to her face until she flinched and stepped back.

He laughed softly. "Let me show you again!" He withdrew the needle and this time bared his forearm and plunged it in again. And once again he let it go through the flesh so that its point showed on the other side. "That is only one of the mysteries which shall be revealed to you. You will be taught the ability to endure great torment and you will be shown how to open your soul to all the delights of the earth!"

She was shaken by the exhibition, having no idea how he'd managed it. She'd seen so-called fire-eaters and sword swallowers at fairs and knew there was some sort of trickery involved. But he was standing there with this giant steel needle protruding through his arm and seeming to suffer no ill effects from the experience at all!

She asked, "Will you try to remember if Helen was here?"

"You would do well to forget her," the thin man intoned. He still had the needle in his arm as he spoke to her. And she felt he'd exerted a kind of self-hypnosis to hide the pain. But there had been no blood!

"I'm afraid I must keep on looking for her," she said.

He removed the needle from his arm, much to her relief, shoved it in the drawer, and said, "I'll want two weeks' money from you in advance," he said. "There is no credit here."

"I hardly expected any. I'll bring you the money as soon as I have unpacked my things."

"Wear something more suitable to this place," the leader of the commune ordered her. "Do you have proper clothing?"

She nodded. "I have some granny dresses and jeans."

"That will be better," Phil Waring said. "I'm accepting you only on a temporary basis. If you stay here any length of time you must, by our rules, become the wife of one of my disciples. I'll give you the time to make your choice while you attach yourself to Tex and his family."

"Very well."

"Come back with the money as soon as you have settled in your room," he warned her again.

"I will," she promised.

"You may go." He turned away from her and gazed out the window. His stooped figure had an aura of evil about it.

He undoubtedly held all the younger members of the cult in awe of him. She turned and quietly made her way from the room. Then she groped her way up the dark stone stairway to the door that led to the large center hall.

She found Dallas waiting for her. The blonde girl asked, "Well?"

"I'm staying as part of your family."

The tall, thin girl in the granny dress said, "Tex has your things up in a room in our section."

It was only then that Rose noticed the earrings the girl wore. They were gold Roman coins. Rose recognized them at once. They had belonged to Helen. A gift from her uncle, they had been a prized possession of hers. How had they fallen into the hands of Dallas?

Chapter Three

Rose was angry and shocked at the discovery. She tried not to reveal her feelings as she forced herself to casually ask Dallas, "Where did you get those lovely earrings?"

The freckled face of the tall girl became wary. "Someone gave them to me. I can't remember who."

"But you must!" Rose insisted, knowing full well the earrings could only have come from Helen, and not understanding why her friend would part with these treasured items.

Dallas was annoyed. "One thing you better learn here is not to ask too many questions. They were a present—that's all I can tell you."

"I'm sorry." Rose realized she had to be diplomatic. She'd have to wait until later and try to find out where the earrings came from when Dallas was in a more confiding mood.

"It's all right!" the tall girl said. "Come along with me."

Rose followed her, feeling that she'd failed momentarily in her attempt to learn what had happened to Helen.

While Dallas might not really know that, she at least knew where the earrings had come from.

They went almost all the way back to the main entrance before taking a side door that led to a stairway. They followed the narrow stairway up two flights and then came to a long corridor with tiny cubicles on either side.

Dallas paused before one of the doors. "In there."

Rose stared at the cubicle. It had poor light from a window high up in the outside wall, a very small window with four tiny panes of glass. The bed was nothing more than rumpled bedclothes on the floor, and looked none too clean. Her bags had been carelessly dumped in one corner. The only other furniture in the room consisted of a chair and a small stand with a glass pitcher of water on it.

"Not very deluxe," Rose said wryly.

"You've got it to yourself, which is more than the rest of us have," Dallas replied stolidly.

"Are all the rooms like this?"

"Except downstairs. That section was done over, but Phil Waring keeps all that for himself."

"I see," Rose said.

Dallas nodded down the corridor. "There's a bathroom along there. And a big kitchen and dining room on the floor downstairs. We have our meals there."

Rose was appalled at the entire pattern of living. But there was little she could do or say. She had exposed herself to this in an effort to find Helen. She would put up with whatever came along until she had succeeded. She felt strongly that the only hope of locating Helen rested with her. To appeal to the authorities would lead nowhere. The leader of this commune was far too crafty to be caught easily.

"Thank you," she said to Dallas, still bothered by the sight of Helen's prized earrings on the tall girl.

"That's okay," Dallas said. "Tex says you're getting special treatment from Phil Waring. You must be paying him well."

"I suppose I am."

The girl shook her head in mock despair. "If I had money I'd pay to get out of here, not to get in."

Dallas walked off and left her. Rose went inside the tiny

room and at once went through her bags to see if anything had been stolen. The first thing she missed was a red blouse she liked and a pair of slippers. She hurriedly went on to the other suitcase and discovered some of her costume jewelery was gone also. Evidently Tex considered himself entitled to payment for checking her bags. He'd helped himself.

It annoyed her without surprising her. No doubt that was how he'd gotten Helen's earrings and later had made a present of them to Dallas. She decided to leave most of her things carefully folded in the suitcases. There were no closets to hang anything in.

Next she straightened out the rumpled bed, which consisted of a mattress on the floor and a couple of sheets and a blanket. When this was done she freshened up after the journey and took the two hundred dollars Phil had requested from her money belt. She left all the rest, except five dollars in single bills and change, in the belt.

Then she went to give the leader his money. She found him talking to a young man with long brown hair and a brown beard. On seeing her the leader dismissed the young man with a few curt words and then gave her his attention.

"You brought the money?" He stretched out a thin hand.

"Yes." Reluctantly she gave it to him.

He took it and counted it carefully. Then his black eyes fixed on her and he reminded her: "You'll owe me another hundred a week from today."

"I know that," she said. "There's something else."

He stuffed the money in his back pocket and frowned. "What?"

"I've seen a pair of earrings on Dallas that I know belonged to my missing girlfriend."

"Well?" His question was coldly put.

"I asked her where she got them and she wouldn't tell me."

The emaciated face of the commune leader broke into a sour smile. "That's the code."

"What code?"

"My orders are that no one talks about where they get things. That only causes trouble. You understand?"

"I'm afraid not. I think if Dallas would tell me where

she got those earrings it could be the first step in my finding my friend."

"You'll ask her no questions. I won't have my ground rules broken. Frankly, I don't care whether you ever find your missing friend."

"But that's one of the reasons I came here."

"You'd better concentrate on the other reasons," he said curtly. "You are now a trial member of the commune and as a member you obey my orders—or get out."

"I see," she said quietly and turned to go.

"There is one other thing, Rose Smith!" the commune leader called after her in a sharp voice.

"What?" she asked, turning.

His emaciated face was grim. "As a member here you are bound to silence—silence about what goes on here. Do you understand?"

"Yes," she said. "I think I do."

"Don't forget it," he warned. "And one other thing. You are not to leave the estate grounds without permission."

"Very well."

"And you are to attend all rituals of the group and take part in them," he went on. "Please remember that."

"Yes," she said in a small voice.

"You may go."

She left him, filled with rage. If ever she'd met a thoroughly evil person, she was sure that it was Phil Waring. The only thing she could be grateful for was that he'd apparently been taken in by her story and underestimated her intelligence. It amazed her that he held people in thrall to him.

She walked out into the courtyard. It was easy to visualize monks parading in this austere area with their leper patients a century ago. This had been their small world and now it was once again a world with boundaries, the world of Phillip Waring's commune.

Rose strolled around to the rear of the monastery and was startled to find there a small cemetery with rows of neat stone crosses. She realized that the inscriptions on the crosses were all in Latin and judged that there must be at least a hundred or more of them. It gave her a strange feeling.

Suddenly she heard footsteps behind her and turned to face the bald, red-bearded addict named Cal. He appeared to be out of his drugged state now and looked quite normal.

He smiled and came a few steps toward her. "You are now in the garden of the dead."

"So it seems," she agreed nervously. "I don't know what the inscriptions mean. I don't read Latin."

"I do," Cal said pridefully. He was dressed in shabby jeans and a flowered shirt that had seen better days. "I once taught romance languages at a private school in California."

She stared at him in awe. "And you've drifted all this way!"

He smiled. "Mostly drifted down, you could say. They call me Cal. You're new here."

"My name is Rose Smith."

Cal's wizened face with its bizarre red beard expressed sympathy. "What trouble got you here?"

"None of my own, I'm looking for a friend who's missing."

"You expect to find her here?"

"This was where I last heard of her."

"What was her name?"

"Helen."

"Helen?"

"Yes." She thought she sensed recognition in the way he repeated the name. Hopefully, she asked, "Do you recall seeing her here?"

He shook his head. "No. But then I'm away a lot. And I'm not always as clearheaded as right now."

It was quite an admission, she thought. He had reconciled himself to his addiction and no doubt to the death to which it would surely lead him.

"You're older than most of the others here," she remarked.

"Yes. I should have died long ago."

"You must be joking!"

"No, I mean it," Cal said very seriously. "I've been ready to die a couple of times, but somebody always sends me to a hospital and saves me."

"Do you have to go on living as you are?"

"Yes."

"Why?"

He looked amused. "Don't ask me why—maybe I like it this way. It's certainly the way of life I chose for myself."

"Don't you realize this man Waring is using you? Corrupting you with drugs and using you?"

Cal gave her a reproving look. "You have it wrong, Rose Smith. He supplies me with the drugs I need and gives me protection."

"In return for which he has you steal for him!"

Cal gave her a weary smile. "Did Tex say that?"

Knowing the code of the group and not wanting to get Tex in trouble, she said, "I don't think so. I just came to that conclusion on my own."

"It sounds like Tex."

"Does it matter? I only said it to try and help you, to make you see how things really are."

The red-bearded wreck laughed softly. "That's the last thing I want; it's why I take drugs. You're wasting your time."

She eyed him with despair. "So it seems."

"And Waring isn't going to like it if you go around trying to reform everyone here."

"Of course you're right," she agreed.

Cal gave her a wise look. "If I were you I'd forget about your friend and move on fast."

"Thanks," she said stubbornly. "But I'm like you. I'm ready to do anything that isn't sensible."

He nodded. "That's where Waring wins out over us. We want to help him."

She sighed. "You never did tell me what the Latin on these various tombstones means."

"They're mostly quotations and testimonials to the glory of God. These were people who lived for others, not for themselves. We haven't much in common with them."

"I'm afraid not."

Cal studied her admiringly. "You're the prettiest thing that has turned up here in months. Most of the other females who've shown up here have been dirty or pregnant—or maybe both."

"The boys don't seem a prize lot, either."

"Watch out for them," he said warningly.

"And Waring?"

"The worst of any of us," Cal said grimly.

"He must have some very strange powers. When I saw him, he stuck a huge steel needle through one of his hands, and then again through his forearm. And it wasn't a trick."

"I know," Cal said. "He always uses that to impress new people. And he sometimes does it at rituals."

"How?"

Cal gave her a smug look. "Let's just say he suffers from a certain disease. And one of the side effects of it is a paralysis of nerves in different parts of the body. The fellows who advertise themselves as human pincushions in the carnivals all mostly have the same disease."

"So that's it!" she said, revulsion in her voice.

Cal glanced around nervously as if afraid someone might have overheard him. "You can guess he isn't anxious for that to get out," he said.

"I understand; you can trust me."

"He's also a sadist," Cal went on. "That's how he fulfills himself. He works it into the rituals. And when he takes LSD, he's at his worst. Keep away from him then."

"He takes LSD?"

"That shouldn't surprise you. I've got an idea that one night he'll take an overdose and walk right off the edge of a monastery parapet. Might be a good thing, though I'd miss him."

"If he were dead you might have a chance to live," she reasoned.

"I don't want it," Cal said sourly. "I'm satisfied just the way things are."

"That's too bad!"

"Thanks! But don't feel bad about it—I don't."

"You're sure you don't remember a Helen?" Rose asked. "She was a pretty girl with a valentine-shaped face, lovely blue eyes, and blonde hair."

"No use asking about her," Cal warned. "You haven't a chance in a hundred of finding her. Every year a lot of kids just drop out of sight and aren't heard from any more. Maybe if you found her now you'd be sorry."

His words chilled her. But she said, "I can't stop looking for her."

"'Everybody's entitled to make his own mistakes."

"So it seems," she replied wistfully. With a nod, she left him standing there amid the crosses. She felt that he'd encountered Helen somewhere.

She entered the monastery and went upstairs, where the dining room-kitchen was a nightmare of screaming children and angry parents. She filled a plate with some of the plain, supposedly organic, food and fled up to the rooftop to eat on the balcony in the open air and sunshine.

Someone was already there: a tiny girl with a ponytail. She wore a short dress belted at the waist.

"Do you mind if I intrude on you?" Rose asked.

The small girl eyed her with snub-nosed indifference. "You already have."

Rose smiled in embarrassment. "That's true. I hope you don't mind." She sat down on a bench.

The small girl shrugged. "What difference would it make if I did?"

Rose adjusted her plate on her lap. "I found some food in the kitchen, but it was so noisy I couldn't stay there."

"The zoo!"

"That's not bad!" Rose said admiringly.

"The food is. You're the one who came with Tex in the hearse, aren't you?"

"Yes. My name is Rose Smith. What's yours?"

The tiny girl eyed her disgustedly. "You think introductions and any of that mean anything here?"

"I don't suppose so," Rose admitted, sighing. "And you're right about the food. It is terrible."

"My name is Susie," the girl said sullenly.

"I'm glad to know you, Susie."

"I doubt it," the girl replied with a bored look on her plain face.

"I'll risk annoying you again by asking what you're doing here," Rose said.

"I'm a kind of servant to the meanest of the families here—the low girl on the totem pole."

"Have you been here long?"

"Since the commune started and that's too long," Susie said.

Rose forced herself to eat the flavorless rice and meat

she'd taken from the kitchen. She wanted to win the girl over. "It's a beautiful spot at least! The view from up here is breathtaking. You can see all of the island!"

"And that's it," Susie complained. "We're not allowed to leave the grounds without permission and he won't give his permission."

"I can't believe it!" Rose exclaimed.

"You'd better," the girl replied grimly. "Oh, he may let you go once in a blue moon if he has some errand for you."

"Everything seems so restricted."

Susie smiled crookedly. "You don't know anything about it; you've just arrived here. There's a war on between the islanders and us. They don't want us here."

"What bothers them?" Rose asked.

"You'll find out soon enough."

Rose put her plate aside and decided to make another try. "If you've been here a year you must have met everyone who's lived in the monastery."

"Just about."

"Then you probably met a friend of mine—Helen."

"Helen?"

"Yes. Does that name mean anything to you?"

"No, should it?"

"I'm positive she was here until about two or three months ago. Then she vanished. I don't know where to. She was brought here by a young man called Jules Bayliss who claimed to be a poet."

Susie's small, plain face was devoid of expression. "There's lots of those poets around. One of them talked me into this place!"

"And you're sorry?"

"I'll say I'm sorry," the tiny girl lamented. "Waring is making slaves of all of us."

"What about Helen?"

"Your friend?"

"Yes. Did you know her or not?"

"If she was here I had to know her. But I don't remember any Helen."

Rose frowned. "Perhaps she changed her name."

"Most everyone does while they are here," Susie said.

"And even when they're on the outside. It's harder for you to be tracked down when you change your name."

"Do you have any memory of a blonde girl with a pretty face?"

"There have been a dozen of them who've come and gone," Susie replied.

"That many?"

"Well, enough of them if you know what I mean. You're not going to find out about her here. You'd be wise to give up."

"I can't."

"Why?"

"I've made myself a pledge to find Helen."

Susie clearly thought that this was idiotic. "And that's why you got yourself into this?"

"Yes," Rose answered.

"You're crazy!" Susie exclaimed.

"I'm sorry you think so," Rose replied. Then she stood up and gazed out across the island. "Is that Dark Harbor far to the right?"

"The cluster of houses on the hill is the beginning of it. You can't see the rest."

"It's a quaint, lovely old place," Rose said. "I don't blame the islanders for not wanting the commune here. Who's responsible for it?"

Susie also stood and looked out at the ocean. "A greedy real-estate operator. I hear there's someone on the island council by the name of Derek Mills who's working on a plan to remove Waring."

"I imagine Waring will fight it. He would have a hard time getting another place like this."

"But this Derek Mills is head of the natural history museum and one of the bigwigs on the island. He may have more influence than Waring guesses."

"Tex said something about it."

Susie eyed her sharply. "You're going to be one of his family?"

"Yes."

"That's not so bad. He's the best-natured of all the family heads. I wish I were assigned to him."

"Couldn't you change?"

"No," Susie said disgustedly. "Waring likes to show his authority when it comes to unimportant members like me. He enjoys making us suffer!"

"Why don't you run away?"

Susie looked bleak. "Nowhere to go. Anyplace I'd find would likely be as bad as this."

Rose felt sympathy for the petite girl. "How long ago did you leave home?"

"Nearly three years now."

"Why?"

Susie stared out at the ocean again, her hands clenching the top of the balcony's stone wall. She spoke without looking at Rose. "My mother was a drunk and my father and she were always fighting. I had to get away."

"Were you the only child?"

"No. I have a younger brother, but he was only five when I left. Too young to be bothered by what was going on."

"Don't you ever think of going back?"

"Yes."

"But you haven't?"

"Things were bad then," the girl said, still staring at the water. "They'd probably be worse now."

"You can't be sure of that. Your parents are probably very worried about you. They've likely been searching for you."

Susie shrugged. "So have the parents of most of the kids here. But we don't want to go back to the kind of homes we had; even this is better."

"Really?"

"Maybe not. But it isn't easy to give up and go back. I know my mother and father never would forgive me."

"You're probably wrong about that," Rose said. "What about the rituals here? Waring told me I was expected to attend them."

Susie turned, again with a bleak expression. "They're really something, especially when Waring gets high on LSD."

"Cal told me some strange things about him," she said.

"Cal knows," Susie assured her. "He may be hooked on hard drugs, but he's been around Waring a long time.'"

"You can't help feeling sorry for him," Rose said.

Susie smiled wryly. "Don't waste your sympathy. Cal is like the rest of us here: he doesn't need it or want it."

"We're all alike, here because we want to be."

"That's it."

"Thanks for telling me what you have," Rose said. "It will help me."

Susie gave her a meaningful look. "I have something else to tell you as well."

"What?"

"Keep your eye open for the ghost."

"Leper Mary?"

The petite girl seemed surprised. "You've heard about her?"

"Yes."

"I've seen her more than once. Are you afraid of ghosts?"

"I'd just as soon not meet one."

"You won't be able to avoid Mary," Susie said. "Most of us have seen her."

"What a tragic story! She was beautiful until leprosy marked her face!"

Susie nodded. "This must have been quite a place in those days."

"From all you say it still is a place of macabre events," Rose said.

Susie nodded. "Watch out for Jeff!"

"I don't think I've met him."

"You haven't. He's been away, but he'll be back tonight."

"What's he like?"

"As bad as Waring," Susie said, her face shadowed. "I'm one of his family. He's great for acid trips and he keeps Waring on the stuff until they're both about half-crazy."

"Doesn't sound pleasant."

Susie's eyes met hers in a warning look. "One of his favorite pastimes is taunting newcomers. So he'll likely be after you. Watch out for him!"

"I'm glad you've told me."

"It's the least I can do. I only wish someone had told me what he was like; it could have saved me a lot of trouble."

"If you hear anything about Helen, will you tell me?"

"You aren't going to learn anything."

"I'm sure she was here," Rose insisted. "Someone must know something."

"Knowing and telling are different things," the petite girl warned her. "I have to go back downstairs. Mind what I said about Jeff."

"I will."

Susie went downstairs, leaving her alone on the balcony. She had the strange feeling that Susie knew a lot more than she was willing to tell. They were all engaged in a conspiracy to make it seem that Helen had never been at the monastery. And Rose knew that she had.

She glanced over the edge of the balcony and saw that some of the commune members still remained in the courtyard. She wondered if she could stand the chaos long enough to learn where Helen was. If she could locate Jules Bayliss, half the battle would be won. But he wasn't at the monastery, either.

With a sigh she sat on the bench again and stared across the island toward Dark Harbor. Perhaps Helen had fled the monastery and taken refuge in the village. That could be why no one wanted to discuss her. Perhaps she could make some inquiries in the village.

Suddenly, the door from the inner stairway opened and Tex appeared. The big black-haired young man looked relieved to see her.

"I've been looking for you everywhere," he said. "I thought maybe you'd run away."

"Not a chance," she said. "Why would you think that?"

Standing there in his cowboy outfit, he looked remarkably youthful. He ran a hand self-consciously through his long black hair as he told her, "It isn't exactly like a resort hotel. I thought you might have been disgusted."

"You forget I came here for a reason. I want to find my missing friend."

He frowned. "That could get you in trouble."

"Why?"

"Waring doesn't like people asking questions. He's already told me to let you know he doesn't want you asking a lot of questions about Helen."

She wondered if he had made this up. And she asked him rather sharply, "Waring said that?"

Tex looked uneasy. "Sure, why else would I say so?"

"I don't know," she replied evenly. "I only know that your Dallas is wearing earrings which belonged to Helen."

"You have to be wrong about that!"

"I recognized them! They were made especially for Helen. They had to be hers!"

"Better forget about it."

"Why?"

Tex scowled. "I gave those earrings to Dallas and I know where they came from. It wasn't from any Helen!"

This startled her. She hesitated a moment and then asked him: "Where did you get them?"

"I can't say."

"Why?"

"I don't have to tell you!"

She eyed him accusingly. "You either stole them from Helen or she gave them to you when she was drugged. Either way it means you knew her!"

"Either way you're wrong," Tex replied angrily. "I don't want to hear any more about it. The ritual is starting downstairs and Waring wants you there. That's why I've been looking for you. He won't like it if you keep him waiting!"

"Suppose I don't go?" she asked defiantly.

"Then you get your walking papers. He won't allow you to stay in the monastery."

"I see. . . ."

"He still isn't sure about you—he thinks you may be a reporter. He's making a special concession in allowing you to stay here."

She sighed, knowing this was probably true. She wanted to ask Tex more about the earrings, but knew it was useless at the moment.

"Where do they hold the rituals?" Rose asked.

"In the grotto."

"Where is that?"

"In the cellar, beyond Waring's main office. I'm supposed to take you down there now."

"Do I need any special preparation for it?"

"Just an open mind," Tex quipped in his likable drawl. "Better come on."

She was wary of this impending experience. She knew that Waring wielded strange power over his followers and she felt that it might be expressed at the rituals. Following Tex down the stairs, Rose descended to the ground-floor level and then down another flight of stairs leading to a sign that directed the reader to the left.

The ritual was under way by the time they reached the cavernous underground room. It was filled with people who squatted on its earthen floor. Tex sat down and motioned Rose to sit beside him.

She at once was aware of several things. The room was filled with clouds of sweet-smelling smoke. Torches were mounted in wall brackets at the rear of a raised platform that served as a stage for Phillip Waring. The room was crowded with the members of the commune, although Rose couldn't pick out any she'd met before because of the dim light.

She and Tex were seated at the left side, about halfway to the stage. She felt some comfort in being with the big Texan, although he had adamantly refused to give her any information about where he'd gotten the earrings.

Phillip Waring was on the stage and he seemed to have taken on a new personality. He wore a purple robe that covered him like a kimono. His eyes seemed peculiarly bright and his pale, emaciated face wore a fixed smile. He faced the group and talked in a weird-sounding language that she could not understand, nor even identify.

Leaning over to Tex, she asked, "What language is he using?"

The black-haired man grinned. "None you'd understand. He's talking to us in strange tongues. You know, like the evangelists do!"

She stared at the figure on the stage and listened to his gibbering. She had heard of certain religious sects who spoke in strange tongues. He waved his hands at the audience and exhorted them for several more minutes.

At about this time she realized that her head was reeling. She suddenly felt panicky, thinking that she might be going to faint. She was experiencing a strange giddiness completely foreign to her.

Again she whispered to Tex: "I feel strange!"

"What's wrong?"

"I think I may be going to faint. My head is funny!"

The big youth chuckled softly. "It's the incense!"

"The incense?"

He nodded in the semidarkness of the crowded room. "Yes. It's some king of Mexican stuff that Waring has brought in. It's put in the torch holders and burns along with them. It gives everyone in the room a kind of temporary high."

She listened grimly; Waring clearly didn't miss a trick. "I hope it doesn't get any stronger. I might pass out."

"Not likely," he said. "You'll get used to it. Being exposed to it for the first time is the worst."

She tried to clear her head and watch a weird routine on the stage. Two assistants, young women in bras and G-strings, carried out a curtained compartment. Like a magician, Waring stepped up to the black curtains of the compartment and opened them to reveal a lovely, dark-haired girl standing inside. She also was nearly nude. He then closed the curtains again and called out three words which Rose couldn't distinguish. After which he drew the drapes open again; where the girl had stood was now a skeleton!

The assistants came forward and lifted the skeleton out of the compartment and carried it across the stage. Waring waited for them, and then wheeled forth a large guillotine on castors. He smiled at the audience while raising the blade of the guillotine several times and letting it fall. When it struck the block below, the shiny steel blade made an ominous thud.

The girl assistants took the skeleton over to the guillotine and placed it on its knees with the skull head under the blade. At this point Waring produced a black bag and placed it over the skull of the skeleton. The girls stepped back and Waring raised the guillotine's blade and it crashed down to sever the sack-covered head from the body.

One of the girls carried out a platter for him to hold, a round silver platter which he showed to the audience. The other girl brought forward the skull in the black sack. She opened the sack as if to place the skull on the silver platter. But when she drew the sack away it revealed instead the gore-splattered head of a human being! The head of the poet with whom Helen had run away—Jules Bayliss!

Chapter Four

Rose let out a startled cry— "That's him!"

It was fortunate that at the same instant the commune members roared their approval of the weird conjuring feat. Rose's cry was lost in the reaction of the group. Phil Waring stood on the stage with the head on the platter, turning it left and right so all might look at it. An evil smile of triumph framed the leader's emaciated features.

Tex had heard her. "What is it?" he asked.

"That's Jules Bayliss, the man who brought Helen here! That's his head!"

"Don't let it get you! It's a phony," Tex said. "We've got a gal here who can make likenesses of anyone or anything out of papier-mâché."

Rose knew she was not thinking clearly because of the effect of the incense, but the head had seemed all too real to her. Yet that wasn't the important thing; her excitement was in seeing the likeness. It proved that Jules Bayliss must have sat for the sculpture and therefore that he was known in the commune.

"Did you recognize the head?" she asked.

Tex nodded. "Yes. I've seen him around."

"Is he here now?"

"No."

"Can't you remember a blonde girl being with him?"

The black-haired youth looked bored. "I didn't pay that much attention. Anyway, he hasn't been around here for a long time. I do know that."

Meanwhile new events occurred on the torch-lit stage. Phil Waring had vanished, along with the platter bearing the head and the two girl assistants. In their place a tall, dark-haired man with a lantern-jawed face and narrowly set cruel-looking eyes ambled forth to stage center. His long black hair fell almost to his shoulders and his bony face wore an ugly, anticipatory smile.

Addressing the gathering, he said, "We have now come to an important moment: the time for administering justice. We know we have certain rules to follow here and that infractions of them bring punishment. Agreed?"

"Agreed," the audience echoed back.

The lantern-jawed man continued to smile and in his harsh voice continued. "Janie Durant broke our rule of mixing with the townies. She left the monastery against the orders of her family and stayed in Dark Harbor for two nights and days. Now she has returned to us. Her punishment must be meted out."

Phillip Waring returned to the stage and took his place at the side of the rangy man, who wore a kimonolike crimson robe similar to the leader's.

Waring had an exultant expression as he said softly, "The punishment is twenty lashes! Ten to be administered by each of us."

They moved to allow the girl assistants to drag out a slim, pretty girl with long brown hair. She wore a halter-type toga which revealed her bare back. She was crying and protesting as the girls swung her around with her back to the group. Then both Phillip Waring and the other man produced riding crops.

A sudden hush fell among the commune members huddled on the floor of the cave. A kind of electric excitement filled the area. Only the sobs and moans of the girl could be heard. Waring and the other man stared at the victim, their whips upraised as if savoring the moment along with the audience.

Then Phillip Waring raised his whip and brought the lash down against the captive girl's lovely back. At once a livid line showed clearly. Before the girl's first tortured screams had been heard, the other man brought his whip down with the same result. Phillip Waring delivered the third lash!

Mercifully the girl fainted after the third lash. And as the end of the punishment approached Rose averted her eyes from the bloodstained back of the victim. When it was over the assistants dragged the unconscious Janie from the stage.

The two men stood, whips in hand, gloating. The members of the commune were silent and Rose felt nauseated. She glanced at Tex and was startled to see a look of satisfaction on his round face. These people actually had enjoyed seeing the torture.

"I have to get out of here!" she murmured.

Tex gave her a troubled glance. "Waring won't like it!"

"I don't care," she said desperately. "I've had more than enough. How long does this go on?"

"The ritual will take maybe another hour," he said.

"I can't stay," she said in a smothered voice and struggled to her feet.

As she left the room, she heard Phillip Waring giving an oration. She groped her way to the exit, aware that she received odd stares from those seated near the door. She made her way up the stairs and then found the center hall. From there she continued out to the courtyard.

Because of the meeting and the obligatory attendance required of all the commune members, the courtyard was empty. It was dark, with only a quarter moon. She strolled in the fresh air, trying to forget the cruel display she'd just witnessed. It was beyond belief that the members of the commune acquiesced to such actions.

She began to understand the hold Waring had over his disciples. They were probably afraid of him as well as beholden to him. She walked to the archway and stood by it, debating whether to flee the monastery. The temptation was great after what she'd seen.

But then she thought about that papier-mâché head. It

indicated she was on the right track. For the likeness to have been made, Jules Bayliss must have stopped at the monastery. And that meant Helen had been there as well. But where were they both now?

This was the question that tormented her. Rose also worried about Dallas wearing Helen's earrings. Either Dallas or her husband knew where they'd come from, but neither would talk. At least not at the moment. There was always the chance she might get them to divulge something later. In the meantime she would remain at the monastery.

She was startled out of her reverie when a cold hand touched her arm. She swung around to look into the pale, ghostly face of the red-bearded Cal, who peered at her out of the dark shadows.

"I thought you were a ghost!" she exclaimed.

"I am, of sorts," the drug addict said dryly.

"You weren't at the ritual?"

"I'm way past that."

"Doesn't Waring resent your not being there?"

Cal smiled grimly. "He knows."

"That awful drug made me dizzy!"

"You should have stayed longer. After a little it dulls the senses and you sit there not questioning anything."

She shuddered. "That must be what was wrong with those others. We witnessed a girl being brutally whipped and none of them showed any revulsion!"

"Waring and his friend, Jeff, are disciples of the Marquis de Sade," Cal said. "Didn't you know that?"

"You're saying they get pleasure from whipping?"

"Most certainly. That is why they find new excuses for administering punishment all the time."

"Why do the commune members put up with it?"

"Many enjoy the spectacle. The others are too frightened to make any protest. If Waring or Jeff saw you leave before the end of the meeting, they'll take you to task for it."

"Let them!" she said defiantly.

"Don't lecture to them about it," Cal advised her. "You might find yourself the next victim. I'm being completely honest with you."

"I appreciate that."

"I can afford to be," he went on with another of his sour smiles. "Waring and I have an understanding."

"Is Jeff his assistant?"

"He is."

"I've been warned against him."

"With good reason—Jeff can be a violent man."

"I had an example of that tonight."

"That is nothing to what he and Waring can do when they've filled themselves with LSD."

"Isn't that dangerous for the mind? I must say Waring looks as if he'd been permanently harmed mentally. He also behaves like it!"

"Be careful what you say about our leader," Cal said warningly. "Especially where the others can hear you. They like nothing better than to carry talk back to him."

"I'll remember," Rose agreed. "Jeff looks as evil as Waring."

"Yet he's only been here a short while."

"I saw something else. Before the whipping Waring put on a kind of magic show."

"His father was a famous magician and an honorable man. The son is not."

"So that's where his equipment and tricks come from."

"Waring uses them to advantage."

"I should say so," she agreed. "He warms his audience up with them." She looked in the direction of the monastery. "I wonder what is going on down there now."

"He ends with the actual ritual," Cal said. "There's a hint of voodoo in it and a lot more magical mumbo jumbo. Most of those in the commune are children in years. Children love magic!"

"That dreadful Jeff," she said. "What's his background?"

"He's from the South. I understand he served a prison term for something or other. Just now he's Waring's right hand. But that needn't last long."

"So I've been given to understand. Tonight I saw Jules Bayliss's head in papier-mâché. It was used in the magic tricks."

Cal's pale face betrayed uneasiness. "I wouldn't know about that."

"I'm sure you do," she said, facing him tensely. "You

are the best of them here in spite of what you've done to yourself. Why don't you tell me what you know?"

"I don't know anything," he said stolidly. "Good night." He withdrew into the shadows and in a moment she couldn't see any sign of him.

It was another frustrating experience. Even Cal, who had shown some friendship toward her, was evidently too dependent on Waring to risk telling her what he knew. He had recognized the name of Jules Bayliss and then rushed away from her as quickly as he could.

She strolled back across the courtyard, hoping she might see Cal, but saw no sign of him. The ghost stories had added to her feelings of fright about the monastery. And she began to worry that Helen might have been abused in some dreadful fashion like the girl she'd seen whipped on the stage a short while before.

The entire atmosphere of the commune was sick. Her only hope was that Jules Bayliss and Helen had left the place before they became too entangled in Waring's evil web. But the sight of Jules's papier-mâché head made her wonder about this. She found herself filled with questions and no answers.

Suddenly the arched front-entrance door of the monastery opened and more than a dozen or so of the commune members trooped out. They were talking among themselves and paid her no attention.

She walked on until halted by a voice that called out her name from behind. "Rose Smith!"

It was spoken harshly. She turned in surprise and found herself looking at the lantern-jawed Jeff. He studied her with a malevolent expression on his long face.

"Yes?"

"You left in the middle of our rituals," he said accusingly.

"I was ill."

"You seem well enough now."

"The fresh air restored me," she told him. "That incense didn't agree with me. I had to escape from it."

Jeff's cruel face framed a sour smile. "No one else has ever complained." He had a nasty-sounding voice and she understood why Susie had warned her against him.

"I can't help that," she said.

Jeff continued to stare at her. His lanky figure loomed threateningly as they faced each other in the darkness. "Waring told me all about you."

"Did he?"

"Yes. You're paying well to be here."

"I have a reason."

He nodded. "So I understand. I consider it a foolish one. You'll never find your friend."

"I disagree," she said. "The head on the platter tonight was the head of the young man she ran away with."

"Is that so?"

"Yes. His name was Jules Bayliss."

The lantern-jawed man smiled coldly. "We have all sorts of people in and out of here every month. I couldn't possibly keep track of all of them."

It was plain he was lying. "I'm sure you could recall him if you tried."

"I didn't come out here to talk to you about that. I wanted to let you know that you're expected to obey the rules. I can't allow you to repeat what you did tonight."

"I see," she said quietly.

His tone was stern. "You're sure you understand?"

She gave him a reproving glance. "You're not suggesting that you might whip me as you did that poor girl tonight?"

Jeff smiled at this, revealing long yellow teeth. "That bothered you, didn't it?"

"You could say so!" she replied defiantly.

He bore down on it. "And that is why you really left the ritual?"

"All of it bothered me. I'm not a child to be impressed by Waring's magic tricks!"

Jeff's smile was cruel. "I'll remember to tell him that."

"You can also tell him I said it for no harm. I'm here for a purpose. He knows what it is and he also knows our arrangement while I'm here."

"Still you have the obligation to obey our rules!"

"I'll remember and I'll try," she said calmly.

Jeff eyed her derisively, "I'd say you'd be wise to do just that." He gave her a parting nod and then went back up the steps and into the monastery.

She stared after him, knowing that she had made at

least one enemy at the commune. Jeff did not approve of her and he'd try to cause her trouble. The one thing which might protect her was the money she was paying Phil Waring. He would not want to shut that off unless he had to.

As she stood there Dallas came up to her. In her Texas drawl she queried, "What did you do to get Jeff's attention?"

Rose turned to her. "I left the ritual."

The freckled face of the other girl shadowed. "He wouldn't like that. No one is allowed to leave the rituals."

"I almost fainted. I couldn't stand that incense or seeing that girl being lashed!"

"You'll get used to those things!"

"Never!" she said firmly.

"You will if you stay here. Those beatings go on all the time!"

"Why?"

"Waring and Jeff like them," Dallas said bitterly. "They don't need much excuse to lash a girl!"

Rose stared at her, wide-eyed. "Why do you stand for it?"

The other girl shrugged. "It happens everywhere! Some groups are worse than this one. A girl takes a chance when she joins a commune. You have to expect some of these things."

She listened with disbelief. The young girls who had fallen into the commune life had become so apathetic and dependent on the men who ruled them that they would put up with this.

"I think you're being victimized. Surely you see that?"

"Then why are you here?" Dallas asked her.

"I told you," she said, her eyes studying the coin earrings that Dallas wore. "I'm looking for someone. Helen!"

"You won't find her," Dallas said. "And if you don't watch out Jeff will single you out for a whipping."

Alarm shot through her. "He wouldn't dare!"

"Don't be all that certain," the tall girl said. "If you stay here you'll do what he says or he'll make you suffer. I know. I've seen it happen before."

"Thanks for the warning," she said. "But he knows I will leave if he tries anything like that."

"You'll go without finding Helen?"

"If it comes to my personal safety," she said. But at the same time she knew that Dallas had made a strong point. She would put up with a lot before she left without her friend. And perhaps knowing that, Jeff and Waring would abuse her as much as they dared.

She said good night to Dallas and went inside. The big central room of the monastery was dark except for one weak light that hung from the high ceiling. She found the steps to the upper floors and made her way up to the cubicle assigned to her.

She went inside and shut the door after her. It had a latch, but no sign of a lock of any kind. There was a drop light from the ceiling with a small bulb. She turned it on as she prepared for bed.

Thus far the entire experience had been a bad one. On the credit side, she had seen Helen's earrings on Dallas and she'd seen the replica of Jules's head. She knew they both had been at the commune. This was supported by the letters she'd received from Helen—but what had happened to the two? Where were they now?

She stretched out on the crude bed. She was also upset by Jeff having singled her out and threatened her. It meant that she was going to have a difficult time at the monastery; she suspected they would try to drain all the money they could from her and then drive her from the commune. It was destined to be a battle of wits between them.

Eventually she fell asleep. The tiny room was cool and she had only a minimum of bedclothes, so she was none too comfortable and slept lightly. She had no idea how long she'd been asleep when she awoke to the sound of the door to her room being opened. She heard its eerie creak and it put her nerves on edge.

Quickly she sat up and stared across the darkness of the small cubicle, her heart pounding wildly. A figure appeared in the doorway—the figure of a woman in a dark habit and wearing a veil over her face. At once Rose recalled the ghost stories and knew this had to be Leper Mary!

The phantom advanced quietly to the foot of her makeshift bed and stood there. Rose was too frightened to move or cry out. She had no idea what the ghost would do next. She stared up at the blurred, veiled figure and waited.

Then slowly and solemnly the phantom lifted her veil and exposed her face to Rose. Rose gasped at the nightmare of scarred flesh, the only recognizable feature two eyes which gazed at her with great sadness. Then the phantom lowered the veil and vanished in the darkness.

Rose experienced trembling and chills. She stared at the door that the phantom had closed after her and tried to decide whether it had been a dream. She knew she'd seen it all, but she would have preferred it to have been a nightmare. The sight of that scarred face would stay with her a long while. Was that the way she usually appeared in her ghostly visitations?

Sleep was impossible, so Rose got up and went to the door, opened it, and peered out into the dark corridor. There was no sign of anyone out there. She closed the door and went back inside. Crossing to the small window she stared out, but it was still too dark to see anything.

The stories of the ghost hadn't been made up, after all. She could now vouch for that. From now on, the old monastery would have a more terrifying atmosphere for her. She paced up and down for a long while, then forced herself to stretch out on the mattress again and wait until a fitful sleep finally came to her.

The next day she sought out Susie. She found her sitting on a grave in the cemetery behind the monastery, her back resting against one of the tombstones as she read a book.

Rose went up to her and said, "I've been looking all over for you."

Susie squinted at her, for the sun shone almost directly in her eyes. "I like to get away by myself," she explained.

Rose glanced back in the direction of the courtyard. "I can understand that. The children make a lot of noise and the girls squabble like a lot of gypsies."

"It's quiet here."

"I wonder they haven't spread out here as well," she said.

Susie smiled. "They don't like all the tombstones. It puts them off."

"It is a pretty somber spot."

"I'll settle for it," Susan said with a grim look on her plain face. "What do you want?"

Rose was taken aback by the girl's bluntness. "I'm sorry if I've interrupted your reading."

"That doesn't matter," Susie said. "I believe in not beating about the bush. I just want to know why you've been looking for me."

Now that she was faced with the question she found herself strangely embarrassed. "You mentioned the ghost to me," she began awkwardly.

"Leper Mary?"

"Yes."

"What about her?"

Rose took a deep breath. "I saw the ghost last night."

The small girl sat up very straight and closed her book. "You did?"

"Yes."

"Tell me when and where," Susie demanded.

"It was some time in the middle of the night. The door to my room opened and she came into the room. I wasn't certain whether I was awake or dreaming."

Susie's eyes questioned her. "Are you sure now?"

"I was awake."

"You're certain?"

"I'd be very surprised if I wasn't."

"Go on," Susie said.

Rose hesitated and then said, "Then the phantom came over to my bed. And after a minute she lifted her veil; I saw her face." Rose paused and shook her head. "I'll never forget that face!"

"Hideous, wasn't it?"

"A mass of scar tissue; only her eyes were normal."

Susie nodded. "Leprosy did that."

"What a horrible disease!"

"What happened next?"

"She covered her face with the veil again and vanished—that was all there was to it."

"Now you know there is a ghost," Susie said.

"I have to believe what I saw," Rose said in agreement. "I wonder why she came to my room."

"You are new here. She always goes to the rooms of

newcomers. I've heard it over and over again. Not likely she'll bother you any more."

Rose frowned. "There was a dreadful sadness in her eyes, as if she meant to tell me something and couldn't."

"Maybe she did."

"You believe in ghosts, don't you?"

"I guess so. I've seen her."

"I never have, at least not up until now."

"And now?"

"I don't know what to think," Rose admitted. "You've heard how clearly it all remains to me. There had to be something."

"It was Leper Mary, looking for the sympathy she didn't get two hundred years ago."

"You're the only one I dare mention it to."

Susie stood up. She was a head shorter than Rose. "Why don't you ask Waring about it?"

Rose stared at her. "Why do you say that?"

"He denies there is a ghost. You might be able to make him change his views."

"I doubt it."

"Why not try? It is time something got to him! Maybe the ghost will!"

"You're making fun of me!" Rose protested.

"Not really," Susie replied.

"Where do I find him at this time of day?"

"The usual place—that retreat of his down in the cellar."

"I want to speak to him, anyway. I can manage to mention the ghost as well."

Susie nodded. "You should."

Rose left her and strolled back to the main courtyard again. It was filled with noisy children and the older members of the commune, who seemed to pay no attention to their progeny. The girls in their granny dresses and other weird outfits and the men with their broad hats and garish clothing presented a strange sight. There was little activity among the grownups, but the children more than made up for this.

With a sigh she stepped inside the monastery and gasped as she almost stumbled over a body on the slate floor. A glance told her it was Cal. The drug addict had apparently passed out after a heavy dose of heroin and no one paid any attention to him.

Dismayed, she stepped past him and hurried down the long, shadowy, central room to the door that led downstairs. She descended the stairs and came to the entrance of Phil Waring's headquarters. Jeff stood in its doorway.

"What are you doing down here?" he asked her.

"I want to see Phillip Waring," she replied.

Jeff gazed down at her insolently. "I don't think he wants to see you."

"I'd prefer to find that out for myself," she said firmly.

Jeff continued to block her way, but at the same time a voice called out from inside, "Who is there?"

Jeff at once looked uneasy and turned to say, "It's the new one."

"Rose Smith?"

"Yes."

"Let her come in."

Jeff looked displeased, but moved aside to let her pass. She went in to the underground room with its large windows facing the ocean. Phillip Waring sat at his desk, bent over a skull. He kept his attention on the skull for a long moment after she'd entered. Then he glanced up at her, a grim expression on his emaciated face.

"This is a two-hundred-year-old skull," he informed her. "It belonged to one of the monks who lived here."

"Oh?"

"We found his bones in an underground chamber that had been missed by everyone else who'd owned the place. When he lived his name was Simon."

"How do you know that?"

Phillip Waring's pasty face broke into a smile. "Easy enough. There was a plate on the coffin where his bones were discovered. The plate was disfigured by rust and mold, but we cleaned it and found his name engraved there. Apparently he was a leader of the monks and a man of much wisdom." The bright eyes below the black brows and slanted forehead stared at her. "I use it as a sort of crystal ball. Do you follow me?"

"I'm afraid not."

He waved a thin hand. "Then I'll be more explicit. I

study the skull and it helps me attune my thoughts. I often solve serious problems with the help of Simon."

"I see," she said carefully, thinking that he was trying to impress her with a rather shoddy theatrical trick.

It was almost as if he had been able to read her thoughts. He rose from behind the desk and came down to confront her as he smiled maliciously and said, "But then you aren't much interested in my magic tricks, or so Jeff has informed me!"

She was at once on guard. "I have an idea he reported my words incorrectly."

There was a nasty glint in the leader's eyes. "He is usually most careful."

"Then he couldn't have understood me," she said.

Phillip Waring paused. Next he said, "I also understand you left the rituals last night. That is strictly forbidden."

"I felt ill."

"You are not to leave a ritual regardless of how you may feel," he said evenly. "Or how much you despise my cheap magic!"

She shook her head. "It was the girl! The way you punished her!"

"That!" he said contemptuously.

"It was cruel!"

The leader of the commune looked angry. "I do not need your advice as to how to operate things here. And I must remind you that you are under the same rules as the others while you remain here."

"At least I can protest what I saw!"

"Is that your only reason for coming down here?"

"No," she said. "Last night I noticed one of the girls here wearing earrings which belonged to my missing friend, Helen."

He frowned. "How can you know that?"

"They were made up specially for her. They were Roman coins given her by an uncle and she had them made into earrings."

"There must be many Roman coins around," he said dismissively.

"But I recognized them!"

"Since this Helen was never here, I fail to see why you

should bother me with this," he said impatiently. "Speak to the girl. She may tell you something."

"She won't," Rose said. "And another thing: the papier-mâché head you used in your rituals last night. It was a likeness of Jules Bayliss."

"You're imagining things!" he scoffed. "That head was designed for the ritual. The artist created it from her imagination. It's not meant to resemble anyone."

"But it does. It looks exactly like Jules. So he must have been here!"

He smiled. "You know your trouble? You have an obsession about all this. Better keep it in hand or it might prove dangerous."

Rose stared at him in consternation. "You dare to suggest that I'm unbalanced?"

"I'm merely offering you good advice."

She looked at him evenly. "Yet it is perfectly all right for you to consult Simon's skull?"

"That is different," he said. "I happen to be psychic and I use the skull as a medium to aid me in my glimpses into the future."

"And yet if I told you that I saw the ghost of Leper Mary last night you'd say I was crazy."

"I'd say that you were too easily impressed. You've heard stories of the ghost from the others and you are too quick to believe."

"No!" she protested.

"I've heard all the stories and they are sheer nonsense," Phillip Waring said.

"But she came into my room. I saw her ruined face!"

"I know the legend. You don't have to bore me with the details."

It was too frustrating. "Unless I have some success in finding my friend I intend to leave at once."

"That is for you to decide."

"You could help me if you wished. I'm sure Helen and that Jules were here, but everyone is covering up the truth."

"Think what you like," he said. "You asked to be allowed to remain here and I've granted you that privilege. I only warn you that you must live by our rules while you are here!"

She was about to reply to this when she heard hurried footsteps on the stairs and moments later a frightened-looking Jeff burst into the room. Ignoring her, he rushed to Waring and cried, "The state police are here! I just managed to get Cal out of the way. He was stretched out in a coma by the door. They are on their way down here now!"

Waring's pasty face became even paler. "What did you do with Cal?"

"Dragged him off into a corner. They didn't see him!"

"What do they want?" Waring demanded.

Jeff shook his head. Before he could reply a stern-looking state trooper came into the room, accompanied by another officer. They paid no attention to Rose or Jeff, but crossed directly to Phillip Waring. She moved slowly away so she was at the other side of the room, standing against the wall.

The first trooper addressed Waring. "We've had more complaints of violence in this place," he said.

Waring assumed a hurt expression. "Why bother me about this?"

"Because I think the trouble is starting here," the first trooper said. "We have had a wave of petty thievery in Dark Harbor and in some of the estates near there. There was no such problem before your group came to the island."

"That's nonsense!" Waring exclaimed. "Why blame it on us? It could easily be a coincidence!"

"We don't think so," the trooper went on. "Now we have been faced with a different sort of crime. A young man was driving along Monastery Road last night and was flagged down by a woman in a weird black outfit. He was alone, but because he was afraid the woman might be in some sort of trouble he stopped his car to see if he could help her."

"What has that got to do with my group?"

The trooper's face was grave and so was that of his assistant. "I'll tell you. The woman produced a gun and shot the young man. He collapsed on the ground and she went through his pockets and stole his wallet and other valuables from him. He got a glimpse of her and claims she wore some kind of horrible mask!"

Chapter Five

Rose listened to all this in growing alarm. She did not dare move for she didn't want to draw attention to herself. If possible she wanted to make it appear she'd overheard very little of what was being said.

She was shocked. And for the first time she wondered if perhaps the legend of the ghostly Leper Mary hadn't been deliberately concocted by Waring to cover up another phase of his thievery. How convenient to be able to blame a ghost for any violence. And how easy for one of the girls—so ready to do Waring's bidding—to don a mask and pose as the leprosy-ravaged beauty of two centuries ago.

Waring said, "That's a ridiculous story!"

"I agree," the state trooper said, "but I have heard rumors about a ghost haunting this place—the ghost of a woman who died here of leprosy. I think you started the story to cover up for this female you've sent out to prey on our people."

Waring's emaciated face wore a look of disbelief. "That's fantastic. No doubt this young man had some sort of hallucination after his accident and fancied the whole thing."

"We don't think so," the trooper stated grimly. "We think it was one of your girls. We're here to do some questioning and I can warn you that we're going to keep a much stricter watch on what is happening here."

"We have a proper lease. And we have our rights to privacy. My lawyer will see that they are preserved."

The trooper gave Waring a disgusted look. "It is always your kind who scream about the law protecting you."

"I mean what I say," Waring insisted, but he was clearly very shaken. Jeff stood in the background, a grim look on his face and carefully kept silent.

The trooper glanced at Jeff. "We know about you," he said. "If we find out you've made just one little mistake we can send you back behind bars for a long while."

"I've done nothing wrong, Officer," Jeff protested piously.

The trooper did the one thing she'd hoped he wouldn't do. He turned and glared at her. Then he crossed the room to confront her.

"What's your name?" he demanded.

"Rose Smith."

The trooper studied her with angry eyes. "Where's your home?"

"New York City."

"Do your parents know you're here?"

"I'm of age. I was working in New York. I made my own decision to come here," she said tremulously.

The trooper sighed. "You should have better sense. You know the sort of outfit this commune is?"

"Yes," she said quietly.

"Where were you last night?"

"Here. In my room upstairs."

The trooper still stared at her, apparently trying to decide if she were the type to don a mask and turn robber. "What do you know about this ghost?"

She hesitated, conscious that all the attention in the room was focused on her. She saw Waring in the distance looking pale and tense. Jeff, standing behind him, had the air of someone ready to run for cover at any moment.

The two troopers watched her with sharp eyes. The silence was frightening.

At last, she ventured: "I think I've seen the ghost."

The trooper frowned. "You saw it? Where?"

"In my room."

"When?"

"Last night."

The trooper looked more annoyed. "Last night, eh? It seems she must have been on the prowl. Can you describe her?"

"Just as you said," Rose told him nervously. "She was in black and when she lifted the veil from her face it was horribly scarred."

"Was that face a mask?"

"I don't know."

"Could it have been?" he persisted.

"I suppose so. I didn't think of it being anything but a ghost."

The trooper smiled coldly. "Quite a ghost when you consider she carries a gun and goes out and intercepts innocent motorists."

"I don't know anything about that."

"Where did this phantom go when she left your room?" he asked.

"I don't know. She seemed to vanish."

"I don't call that much of an answer!"

"I'm sorry."

The trooper turned to Waring. "I'm going back upstairs to hold a general questioning. I intend to find out who shot and robbed that young man."

"Question whomever you like," Waring replied. "We're always anxious to cooperate with you fellows, whatever you may think."

The trooper glared at the leader of the commune. "I'll tell you what I think, Waring. I think you're rotten and any of these youngsters who've fallen under your spell are in trouble."

Waring was deathly pale. He shrugged. "You're entitled to your opinion."

"I know your kind," the trooper continued. "And sooner or later you'll make a mistake; I hope this may be it. If we don't get you this time count on our being back again."

"Good luck, Officer," Waring said tautly.

The trooper turned to Rose again. "If you have any sense, young woman, you'll head back to New York and your job."

"Thank you," she said quietly.

The two troopers left the room abruptly and went up the stairs. Waring motioned to Jeff to follow them. He nodded and slunk off after the troopers. Waring made no attempt to speak for a moment. He crossed to the window and stared out at the ocean grimly for a few seconds.

Then as if a storm had been gathering inside him he spun around, his emaciated face distorted in anger. "Scum!" he screamed wildly. "Dirty scum! How dare they come here and threaten me!"

She said quietly, "If you don't mind I'll go now."

"Wait!" he commanded.

"Yes?"

"I didn't give you permission to leave." He seemed ready to vent his anger on her.

"I didn't think you'd mind my going."

"Oh, didn't you?" he inquired sarcastically. "Well, maybe you were wrong!"

She saw that he was in a mood to which she must cater. "I'll stay if you wish," she replied submissively.

"Why did you remain here in the first place? Eavesdropping!"

"I was afraid they'd stop me if I started out of the room."

He stared at her moodily. "Probably you were right. At least you answered them correctly about the ghost."

"I told the truth."

"All right, let it go at that," Waring said. "There's nothing to that story about the woman who held that man up coming from here. You understand that?"

"Yes."

"I want you to forget everything you heard down here!"

"I will!"

"Leaders of new thought are always harassed," he ranted, pacing up and down. "That is why they won't give me any peace. They want me off the island."

"Perhaps you'd be better off to leave."

"No," he said quickly. "I've paid for three months' use of the monastery and I have options to renew the lease. I intend to hold that realtor to them."

"But if they continue to bother you?"

"They'll not drive me out. I promise you that. You can leave now if you like."

She didn't wait for a second time. Knowing how erratic he was, and that any small thing could change his mind in a matter of seconds, she made her way quickly to the exit and mounted the dark stairs. It had been a strange experience, but at least she had one satisfaction: she knew that the police watched the monastery closely. And this would have a tendency to keep Waring from becoming too brazen in his behavior.

She reached the central room and walked along its cool, shadowed length. Outside, the police still questioned the other girls. Rose wondered if one of them might really be impersonating the ghost. Was it some girl in a mask she'd seen in her room? She doubted it. She had almost felt the eerie presence of the phantom figure. And the face had been more horribly real than a mask could be.

But perhaps there were two ghosts—the real one and a girl playing the part. If Waring had sent a girl out to rob, he was overreaching himself. Not content with sending the drug-addicted Cal out on thieving raids, he was apparently expanding his predatory assaults on the islanders.

She was near the end of the room and about to go outside when a figure darted from the shadows and grasped her by the arm. She gave a small, frightened cry before she saw it was Cal.

"What are the police after?" he whispered hoarsely.

"There was a holdup near here last night."

"Last night?"

"Yes."

"No one mentioned me?" he asked nervously.

"No, except I heard Jeff say you were in a coma and he dragged you away before the police found you."

"All right," Cal snapped impatiently. At that moment Rose realized that he was trembling and perspiring. "What else?"

"A woman committed the robbery."

"A woman?"

"Yes. According to the victim she was dressed like a nun and when he saw her face it was scarred like the ghost of Leper Mary."

Cal seemed surprised. "So that's it."

"You know what's going on?"

"It doesn't matter," he told her.

"The police are questioning all the girls now."

"Are they?" He no longer seemed interested or even the least bit worried.

"Yes. They questioned me."

"You were in no danger."

"I thought I was for a minute or two."

Cal looked satisfied. "They won't find the robber."

"Why?"

He smiled thinly. "Ever try to capture a ghost?"

"Ghosts don't carry guns!" she protested.

"Maybe this one does."

"You know something, don't you?" she asked.

"Why do you say that?"

"It's just the same as before. You know, but you don't dare say anything. You're afraid if you do he won't give you the drugs you need."

"Why should I deny that?"

"Haven't you any pride?"

"None."

She sighed and turned away from him. "I can't even be sorry for you," she said dully.

"One thing, though—I do want to be your friend."

"You haven't worked at it very hard," she told him bitterly.

"I'll do what I can whenever I can. Just remember that."

She faced him again as they stood in the cool shadows. "Then why won't you help me find Helen?"

The red-bearded man shook his head. "I can't!"

"Because you're afraid of Waring. I know he and that Jules robbed her of her money. Even so, I'm only interested in saving her."

Cal looked at her earnestly. "You'd be better off to forget her and think of yourself!"

"I can't do that!"

"You'll have to face up to it sooner or later," he warned her. "You're no match for Waring or Jeff or any of the rest of them."

"Helen was here. Most of you know it," she said. "Yet you won't tell me where she is now."

"You only think she was here. You'd be wise to believe what you're told. Mind your own business and leave the monastery."

"No!"

Cal lifted a trembling hand in warning. "Stay long enough and Waring will get a hold on you. Then you won't be able to get away!"

"How can he get a hold on me?"

"He'll find a way," Cal warned. "You're attractive. He'll have some use for you. He'll get you on to some kind of drugs and you'll be hooked!"

"I won't be as easy a mark as you," she told him.

Cal laughed bitterly. "Don't think I'm the only one he's trapped. Just because I'm a horrible example you mustn't forget about the others."

"Thanks for the good advice. I still intend to stay here until I find out what I want."

She went outside and saw that the troopers were still there. She kept close to the building and dodged around the corner to the cemetery. She walked the length of it, going as far as she could, until she came to the very end of the courtyard wall.

This area was cloaked in a brooding, eerie silence. She stood thinking about it all and wondering what would happen next. It was then she noticed the black painted door that seemingly led into the monastery's cellars. Curiosity urged her to go over and try the door handle. It turned easily. She opened the door and was confronted by a steep flight of stone steps.

Leaving the door open she ventured downward. As she gradually descended into the dark she had difficulty adjusting her eyes to the gloom. She hesitated on the bottom step and waited until she was able to distinguish her surroundings. Giant hogsheads were piled in one corner with a passage extending to the right. She decided to follow the passage.

A pinpoint of light seeped down from the open door at

the head of the steps. She started cautiously along the passage and saw a door to the right. She halted and tried the door and found she could open it. Inside there was a table with a candle in a stone holder. She had matches in her pocket. She lit one and touched it to the wick of the candle.

A flickering tongue of flame gave the room a modest amount of light. She studied her surroundings and gasped as she saw a dried-up face beneath a monk's cowl in a distant corner of the room. The wizened creature sat in a chair and wore a gray habit. One glance told her it was a mummified figure.

Clutching the candle holder, she turned and fled the room, terrorized. She'd barely reached the corridor when she heard the door above slam closed. Except for the small, wavering flame of the candle she was now in total darkness. Worst of all she had the frightening feeling she was not alone. Then she heard a footstep—stealthy, but close behind her.

She didn't dare turn round. Instead she ran ahead, trying to keep the candle flame from going out. Her terror was increased by her hearing someone behind her. She reached what seemed like a dead end and her heart sank! Then she found a rough opening to the left. She raced along this and came to another set of stone steps that led downward. Without hesitation she took them, wanting to escape her phantom pursuer.

She stumbled at the bottom of the steps and sobbed fearfully. The candle and holder were jolted out of her hand and the candle went out. She ran on in the darkness, with no idea of where she headed. She could no longer tell if she was being followed or how close her pursuer might be! She wanted only to escape!

The passage became uneven and she had difficulty in keeping her footing. She stumbled every few steps. Ahead, she heard a rumbling. It was like the sound of muted thunder and the passage vibrated with it!

There was a sudden dampness in the air. She came to a kind of turn and all at once she saw light ahead—the most welcome sight she'd ever seen! She struggled forward.

The lighted space loomed ahead, and then she saw the

spray of waves as they dashed against the rocks. She reached the mouth. The monastery cellar led to the beach! She realized that when the tide was high the mouth of this tunnel must be completely blocked, with the water extending far into it under the ancient monastery.

She turned and stared back along the passage, speculating on who or what followed her. And she knew she had neither the courage nor the desire to brave the passage again.

What to do? She gingerly edged out among the huge boulders which screened the mouth of the tunnel from view. She saw, with mounting apprehension, that she was trapped on a narrow rocky section of the shore. There could be no escape by walking along the beach. On either side of jutting rocks there was only the boiling surf. The tide sent waves crashing. White spray leaped many feet into the air.

It took Rose only a moment to realize that she had two choices: risk going back along the tunnel before it filled with the incoming tide or climb up the almost vertical face of the cliff, which rose perhaps fifty yards at this point.

She moved cautiously out among the boulders and was at once drenched by an incoming wave. She stumbled back, half-stunned and feeling more than half-drowned. She could not remain safely at the beach level and she dared not go back into the passage again. She did the only thing left to her. She clambered up on the face of the cliff.

She'd seen motion pictures of mountain climbers edging their way up steep cliff faces, reaching for a small crevice here, a ledge there, moving to the left or right. It was always a tortuous business, fraught with the terror of a climber losing his footing and falling to an agonizing death.

Now she faced the same test. And she had no preparation for it. No equipment to test the rock, no joining rope to another climber to help her if the worst did happen. And she was soaking wet.

Breathing heavily, she managed to climb a dozen feet or so until she was above the spray. Clutching the stony face of the cliff she glanced down apprehensively and saw the angry waves. She quickly averted her eyes and looked upward. She knew if she glanced down again for even a few seconds she would faint and drown in the melee of those pounding waves and sharp rocks.

She closed her eyes for a moment and tried desperately to relax. Then she looked up and saw that the face of the cliff seemed to rise to a dizzying skyscraper height!

The easy way would be to cry for help. But there wasn't a hope that she could be heard above the crashing of the waves. And this cliff front was on the far side of the monastery, so there wasn't apt to be anyone on the ground above.

Her fear drove her upward. She went on, a foot at a time. Sometimes she gained only three or four inches. But she moved on toward the top. She learned just how narrow a ledge she could risk placing her weight on, how wide a crack in the rocks need be for her to press her fingers in it and later her toes. Her fingernails broke and her sandals had long since been abandoned.

Once a moss-encrusted ledge had seemed stronger than it actually was. It crumbled under her and almost sent her plunging downward into the ocean. She cried out and fought desperately until she managed to grip the rock face again. When she did she lay limp against it, sobbing for long minutes before she moved.

She finally found herself no more than seven or eight feet from the top of the cliff. But from there on up the surface was completely smooth. Worse than that, it seemed almost impossible to climb.

She wept! To come so far and fail was a heavy blow. She could not remain on the ledge for any length of time. Night would come and she would fall asleep from sheer exhaustion and topple down to the death she'd fought to escape.

She decided to cry out for help. She was far above the waves and so with luck her voice might be heard. She cried out again and again. Her voice became hoarse and she was conscious of her miserable, wet condition.

What to do if no one answered? She examined the face of the cliff again and tried to chart a course. But it was no use.

And then, just as her despair became overwhelming, she

heard someone on the ground above. She looked up and saw the face of a young man peering over the edge.

"Help me!" she cried.

"I will," he said. "Just hold on for a moment; I'll be back."

She closed her eyes and wept tears of joy. Hugging the cliff she waited. Then she heard footsteps again and knew he had returned.

"All right?" he called down.

"Yes."

"I'm dropping a rope to you," he said. "Tie it around you and then brace your feet against the cliff as I gradually drag you up."

"Thank you!" she cried.

"Don't worry about thanks. Get that rope tied tight and properly. Don't make a slip knot or the pressure will be too tight around you. Try a granny. Do you follow me?"

"I think so."

"There can't be any question," he said. "Make sure!"

She grasped the rope and fumbled at it. The first time she failed miserably, so she tried again and still wasn't satisfied.

He called out again at her third try. "Perhaps we'd better find another way."

"No," she said, frantic that he might leave her. She knew she couldn't face waiting on the ledge alone any longer.

"Still having trouble?" he called down to her.

"I think I have it tied well enough now," she said.

"Ready to try?"

"Yes."

"Remember if the rope slips or breaks it will be your life," he warned her.

"I know. But I can't stay here any longer. Please start me up."

"Right away," he said.

She followed his instructions. As he pulled the rope up she braced her feet against the cliff. It was not a fast or an easy ascent, but within a few minutes he grasped her by the arms and lifted her up onto the grass of the plateau.

She lay there, breathing heavily, her heart pounding from all the pent-up fear.

"That was close."

"I know," she gasped.

"I didn't like taking the risk, but I couldn't leave you there."

"You did right."

"How in heaven's name did you get in that predicament?"

She regained control of her breathing. "I was in the cellar of the monastery and found my way to the beach by an underground passage. Then I realized I was caught out there by the tide."

"You were in the monastery?" Even in her spent condition she recognized a wary note in his voice.

She glanced up at him. "Yes." She saw that he was young and handsome with brown, wavy hair. He wore a sport coat and slacks.

He frowned. "Why didn't you go back through the tunnel?"

"I was afraid. I felt sure I'd lose my way. I only stumbled onto the passage by accident."

"I see," he said. He glanced toward the cliff's edge. "You actually made your way all the distance up to where I found you?"

"Yes," she sat up. She felt embarrassed at the state of her clothes.

His eyebrows raised. "But that was an incredible feat! Incredible!"

"I hadn't any choice."

He stared at her, still startled. "I can tell you this: I don't believe anyone has ever climbed that cliff face before."

"I'd never try it again," she said wanly.

"Remarkable," he said. "I'm glad you made it."

"Thanks to you," she replied, rising to her feet.

"Did you hurt yourself?"

Her smile was bitter. "Nothing more than a few broken fingernails and my toes scraped. Plus a few odd bruises and cuts."

"You'll recover from all that."

"Easily. I'm sorry I'm such a sight. My clothes were all

right before I started up the cliff. A wave drenched me before I really began that awful climb."

He was polite, but not friendly as he said, "Just be glad you're still alive."

"I am." She saw that they were to the left of the monastery. Its courtyard wall loomed above them and she judged that they were probably opposite the cemetery. The main courtyard was on the other side of the building.

"You are one of Waring's group?" he asked.

"Yes."

He stared at her as if he found this hard to believe. "Have you been here long?"

"Only a few days."

"So it only took you a short while to get into serious trouble," he said grimly.

"I'm afraid so."

"Do you plan to remain?"

"I've joined the commune for a few weeks."

"Do you think you will enjoy it?"

"I'm not sure. Why do you ask?"

He hesitated. Then he said, "There are rumors on the island that the commune isn't very desirable."

"Oh?"

"I can't tell you any more than that," he said. "But many of the islanders would like to see them out of the monastery and off the island."

"I think Phillip Waring has a lease on the property."

"Only a short-term one for a few months and I think the owners will refuse to rent it to him any longer."

She smiled ruefully. "I'm sorry, but it seems I'm one of the enemy."

"So it appears," he said frankly.

Her eyes met his. "And now I owe you my life? How do I pay you for that?"

The young man looked embarrassed. "No need to worry about it. I'd do it for anyone."

"Well, I'm sure you would," she said. "But I'm still grateful."

He blushed. "You'll forgive me. You seem too nice to be one of the monastery crowd."

"Is that a compliment?"

"It's meant to be one," he assured her.

"I'll remember that."

He frowned. "You probably know Waring is having some trouble with the police."

"They were at the monastery when I left."

"I think they've just gone," he said. "But they could return at any time."

"So I gather."

"If you have any trouble I'd be willing to help."

"Thanks," she told him. "I wouldn't want to impose on you."

"I'd like to help you," he said seriously. "My best advice would be to leave the monastery and that gang."

"You consider them all that bad?"

"I'm afraid so. Still it is bound to be a matter of opinion."

"Yes." She was fully recovered from her ordeal now, except for her minor injuries and torn clothes. "I will think about leaving the commune."

"Do," he urged her.

"I suppose I must walk back to the courtyard entrance and change my wet things."

"Of course. I'll walk you there," he said. "I have a car parked by the main highway."

"I see."

"I sometimes drive down this way and enjoy the view," he told her as they strolled along. "It's the best of any part of the island."

"Lucky for me you came along."

"Someone else would have."

"I doubt it. I know very little about the island. I came straight to the monastery from the ferry."

"So you've just seen Dark Harbor and the road here?"

"Yes."

"There's quite a lot more to see. You should enjoy it while you are here."

She gave him a quick glance. "Phillip Waring doesn't encourage us to mingle with the islanders or travel about on our own."

"I've heard that. Why?"

She sighed. "I guess he wants complete control of us all."

"Are you content with that?"

"We agree to it when we become a member of the commune."

The young man gave her an embarrassed look. "What is all this I hear about families and wives?"

"The females are assigned to families led by various males. Under the system the male is bound to have more than one wife."

He looked even more embarrassed. "None of the unions are legal, of course."

"Unless multiple common-law marriages are recognized in this state," she replied demurely.

"They aren't."

They neared the entrance to the courtyard. Rose said, "I'd like to say that I'm not officially attached to any family. I'm sort of under the wing of a friend. But I'm not a wife."

The man walking beside her seemed happier. "I didn't think you'd be the type to go in for that sort of thing."

"I'm not claiming to be holier than the rest of them. The idea didn't appeal to me."

"Good for you."

She halted at the open archway to the walled courtyard of the monastery and held out her soiled and scratched hand. "May I thank you again?"

He took her hand and held it a moment. "I'm glad to have done something useful for the day. So often one doesn't."

She smiled. "That's a nice way to feel about it. I hope we meet again."

"So do I," he said awkwardly. He glanced toward the monastery. "Perhaps if you decide to leave this place I'll see you in Dark Harbor."

"It's possible."

"I'll hope for that."

With a nod he left her and walked toward his car. She watched him get in it and drive away in the direction of Dark Harbor.

Only then did she realize, with a feeling of dismay, that she hadn't given him her name nor he his. It would be impossible for her to seek him out if she wanted his help. And he seemed to know a good deal of what took place on Pirate Island. For instance, he'd been aware of the police calling at the monastery and questioning Waring.

She liked the young man's looks and his way of talking. She also felt that he was someone important in the island's affairs. He'd made it plain that the commune was anything but popular with the natives. For this she couldn't blame them.

Aware of her wet and miserable condition she turned and walked back through the archway. She would go straight upstairs and change her clothes, after taking a hot bath. Everything she had on was ruined. As she neared the arch she saw that someone stood by one side of it. Someone had lurked there during her talk with the young man and watched her. It was Jeff.

She lifted her chin to a defiant angle as she passed him. She didn't want him to think she was frightened of him. But she was.

"Making some friends?" he asked sarcastically.

She turned. "What difference does it make to you?"

"None to me," he said, a mocking smile on his ugly face. "It might to Waring."

"He doesn't own me!"

"That could be a matter of opinion," Jeff told her.

"I don't want to discuss this with you," she said. "If he has any complaints he can make them to me himself."

"He will," Jeff told her ominously. "I can promise you that."

Chapter Six

Knowing too well that Jeff was her dedicated enemy and anxious to cause her trouble, she felt a chill run through her at his words. But she marched on, not willing to let him know how afraid she was of him. She regarded him as pure evil, perhaps worse than Waring.

As she neared the monastery entrance, she passed Tex and a stout helper painting the black hearse with gay flowers and other designs. Tex paused in his painting to stare at her with wide eyes.

"What happened to you, someone run you through a mangle?" he wanted to know.

She smiled grimly. "I had a bad experience."

"I never saw anyone look like that from acid before," the big youth said doubtfully.

"This wasn't from acid," she told him. "I was caught at the bottom of the cliffs. I had to climb up."

Tex gasped. "I don't believe it!"

"I did."

"You must be part cat."

"Maybe." She nodded toward the hearse. "Do you think your painting is going to improve it?"

Tex turned his gaze to the hearse. "Don't you like it?" he asked, obviously let down.

"Perhaps after you finish with it," she said diplomatically.

"Yeah, some more designs will make a big difference. I want the islanders to stand up and notice this old girl when she whizzes by!"

"You needn't worry about that," Rose assured him and went on inside.

Hurrying upstairs she went to her room and changed into a bathrobe, then she walked down the hall to the large bathroom which served the floor. Fortunately it was empty and she was able to take a shower in comparative peace. Feeling much better she returned to her room and put on a new outfit.

Thinking about the adventure in retrospect she realized how easily she could have been killed and how fortunate she was that the considerate young man had come along. She also wondered about who had pursued her in the cellars.

She went to the kitchen early and prepared a hamburger and some french fries. Then she went up to her room again to eat. The noise and turmoil in the kitchen was too much!

She was finishing her meal when there was a knock on her door. She opened it and a young man dressed in an outfit of multicolored suede patches ambled in. He was a small youth with a rather weak face and dark complexion.

He eyed her plate and looked surprised. "You eat here?"

"Why not? I find the kitchen downstairs too noisy," she said, wondering who he was and why he'd intruded on her.

"The kitchens are noisy," he said. He drew a cigarette from a package he'd taken from his hip pocket and offered her one.

She refused. "Thank you, no."

"You don't smoke?" This seemed to startle him.

"No."

Hopefully, he asked, "What about grass?"

She shook her head. "No."

His eyebrows raised and he smiled at her. He had a completely unattractive face and his smile wasn't really pleasant.

Lolling against the wall he drew on his cigarette and exhaled two spirals of blue smoke. "Go ahead with your meal. Don't let me bother you."

She was ready to play along with whatever game he had in mind. He obviously hadn't come to her without a purpose. She sat down at her plate again and waited for him to say something.

He did. "My name is Frank."

She looked up at him. "Mine is Rose."

"I know that," he said, studying her in a lazy way. "Tex told me he picked you up coming over on the ferry."

"That's where we met," she admitted. "And I think to be fair I'd say we picked each other up."

Frank smiled. "I like a girl who is aggressive."

She faked a smile for him. "That's me! Little old aggressive!"

"Tex says you're here because you're looking for someone."

"Right!" She put the plate aside.

"And you're one of the family, but not his wife."

She smiled bleakly. "The news gets around."

He tapped the ash from his cigarette. "I can understand that."

"Can you?" she asked. She began to think that she didn't much care for Frank.

"Sure," he said complacently. "Tex is a kind of slob; you need a different type. You want a guy who knows his way around. Right?"

"I find everything you're saying fascinating," she told him, feeling that this wasn't really committing herself one way or the other—at least she hoped not.

Frank took this as a compliment. He smiled and drew in on his cigarette again and made a show of exhaling. He took his time. After he'd admired the two spirals of smoke, he said, "I think you ought to make a change."

"Do you?" she asked cautiously. By this time she had a good idea of what his offer was going to be.

"I do," he said, fixing his eyes on her. "I think you should join my family. You can be my number-one wife.

I've got no ties like Tex. No Dallas to keep beating up any females who try to take over from her."

"Does Dallas do that?"

"Try moving in on her and see."

"I'm really not interested."

He waved his hand. "Well, there you are. I can protect you and maybe help you find that missing girlfriend of yours."

"Honestly?"

"Do you think I'm a guy who talks big with nothing behind it?"

She did, but she didn't say so. Instead, she said, "Your offer is flattering. But what about your number-one wife?"

Disgust registered on Frank's weak face. "She's no problem."

"No?"

"No. You were at the ritual the other night?"

She nodded. "I was."

"You saw the girl who was whipped on the stage?"

"Yes."

"That was her! That was Greta! She'd just got back from playing around with some townies!"

"I felt very sorry for her. Was she badly hurt?"

"She likes to be beaten," Frank said scornfully. "Didn't you get wise to that? She moaned most of the night. But yesterday she was able to crawl around. And today she's down there again shooting acid with Waring and Jeff. Those three are always going on highs together!"

Rose was astounded. "She's addicted to acid?"

"And pills," he said. "That's all she lives for. She doesn't care about me or herself or anyone."

"I see."

"I'm going to get rid of her anyway," Frank said. "Let Waring look after her. She spends most of her time with him. I'm going to take me on a new wife. And you could be the lucky girl!"

Covering up the revulsion she felt for the whole business, she forced a bleak smile. "Well, that's very nice of you. I'll want a little time to think it over."

"Why?"

"Because it will have a bearing on my life," she said. "I

think a marriage is a marriage even in this place. And even whether it is without benefit of clergy."

Frank eyed her with wonder. "You got principles?"

"I hope that doesn't turn you off me."

He shrugged. "I guess not, but I don't want you to take too long deciding about us."

"I won't," she said with a forced smile. "It's just that the idea is so new to me."

"Sure," he said. "I've been thinking about it every since you came here. I like your type. Don't sell me short. I'm not so pretty, but I got ideas! Right?"

"Right," she said solemnly.

"One day I'm going to have a setup like this of my own," he went on. "Anything Waring can do I can do better. I'll have all the dumb guys and chicks working for me just as he does."

"I can tell you have a bright future."

"Well"—he shrugged modestly—"a guy wants to get somewhere!"

"I admire that. You said you might be able to help me find Helen, my girlfriend. That interests me greatly. I'd appreciate anything you can do."

Frank looked wary. "Yeah," he said. "Maybe I can work on that."

She frowned. "But you said you already knew something!"

He lifted a hand in protest. "I didn't exactly say that. I think maybe I saw her. She was here with a tall, thin guy who was always spilling out poetry! A dope!"

"Jules Bayliss!"

"Yeah. That was his name."

As much as she disliked and distrusted this brash young man, she was all eagerness now. The hope that he might be able to solve some of the mystery was enough to make her listen to him.

Frank looked smug. "I remember them. She was a blonde."

"Yes, very pretty."

"Sure. Waring and Jeff had her down there talking to them. And she made quite a few trips into Dark Harbor. That Jules had an old car and he drove her."

"She went there for money. Waring talked her into draining her bank account and giving it all to him."

"Yeah?"

"Of course they all deny she's ever been here. You're the first one to say yes."

"Well, you're entitled to the truth."

"Where is she now?"

"That I don't know," Frank confessed. "One day she and Jules went away in the car and never came back."

"You're sure of that?" Rose asked desolately. If this were true, and no one knew where they had gone, she was wasting her time at the monastery. Endangering her life for nothing!

"Yeah. They drove off one afternoon. I think they had some kind of a fight with Waring."

"Probably about the money he bilked out of them!"

"Sure," Frank said, studying his cigarette ash. "I wouldn't worry about her if I were you. They could be anywhere by now. Lots of those guys head for the West Coast."

She stared at him worriedly. "You think that's where they went?"

"Maybe. Who knows?"

Rose got to her feet and took a step toward him. "Did you talk to either of them when they were here?"

Frank's weak face looked shifty. "Yeah! Sure, I talked to them."

"What did they say?"

He shrugged. "What does anyone say around here?"

"This is important to me," she told him, her voice trembling. "How did she look? Was she well? Did she seem to like this kind of life?"

Frank considered. "I guess they weren't laughing all the time, but they looked as if they were getting on all right. She spent a lot of time down talking to Waring. I'd say he was selling her some bill of goods."

Rose asked pointedly, "What did Helen say to you?"

"To me?"

"Yes!"

"I don't know," he replied falteringly. "It wasn't important to me at the time. I didn't pay much attention to her.

She was just another stupid blonde broad. You know how it is."

"I'm afraid not," Rose said desperately. "It would mean a great deal to me if you could recall even one thing she said to you."

He rubbed his chin. "Once she asked me for a cigarette."

"And?"

His eyebrows lifted. "I gave it to her! That was it!"

"Nothing else?"

"Not that I can remember."

Rose couldn't be sure whether he was telling her the truth or merely a lot of lies to strengthen his case with her. It was all too likely that he pretended to know more than he did. But she dared not give up questioning him, since he offered her hope.

"What about the man? Jules?" she demanded. "What did he say to you?"

"He spouted a lot of crazy poetry," Frank said in disgust.

"He must have had a normal conversation with you at least one time," she protested.

"He was never normal. Not that guy!"

"Did he mention the West Coast?"

Frank frowned and snubbed out his cigarette. "He talked about having been out there."

"And he said he was going back?"

"He said he liked the climate better."

"What about the day he and Helen drove away?"

"I hadn't seen him to talk to for a couple of days, but someone told me he and Waring had a row."

"You don't know what about?"

"Waring never tells anyone anything. You ought to know that."

"I'm just trying to get some idea of where they might have gone and whether there is any chance of their coming back."

"I don't know," Frank said nervously. "Anyway, I got to go now. I have to meet somebody."

"We'll talk again," Rose said.

"Sure, I'll be back for my answer. You'd better move

out of here. You're not going to get anywhere with that Dallas around."

"Maybe you'll remember more later."

"Yeah, maybe," he said. And he left.

Rose watched him leave with a feeling of despair. She could tell that he'd hurried off because of her questions. Perhaps it had been a good move on her part; otherwise he might have tried to force himself further on her. She pictured being clutched in the horrid little man's arms and fighting him off. That would have been unpleasant!

On the other hand, his nervousness suggested that he had lied to her. That he didn't have any significant information about Helen and Jules. He might even have made up the things he had told her, yet there had been a ring of truth in his words.

Unwilling to remain in the small, humid room she went out and took the stairway to the upper level of the monastery. Walking out onto the balcony she saw that it had grown dark for so early in the evening. Then she saw Susie seated on her usual bench.

Rose went over to her and asked, "What does this mean?"

Susie glanced up at the heavy gray clouds. "I'd say we were in for a thunderstorm. We get some dillies here!"

"I can imagine! It's so high! And right on the ocean!"

"It's bad." Susie drew her knees up and clasped her hands around them as she sat on the bench.

"I'm terrified of bad electrical storms," she confessed, starting down at the ocean.

"The thunder rolls through the monastery like nothing you ever heard before."

Rose studied the cliffs at the point where she'd been rescued. The memory of the nightmare climb mingled in her mind with the memory of her handsome rescuer. Again she wished that she had found out who he was. It had been a day of conflict and turmoil. She was in no state for a thunderstorm.

After a moment, Rose turned to Susie and said, "What have you been doing all day?"

"Helping in the kitchen," the other girl said disgustedly. "I hate it."

"I don't blame you."

Susie gave her a knowing look. "I was on my way up here a few minutes ago and I saw company leaving your room."

Rose was startled. "You mean Frank?"

"Yes. How well do you know him?"

"That's the first time I've ever met him. He came into my room uninvited."

"Sounds like him," Susie remarked grimly.

"You don't like him?"

"He's scum!"

"I was dubious about him."

"Plain scum!"

"He said that Greta lives with him."

Susie scowled. "Greta lives with anybody!"

"He claims she and Waring take acid trips together."

"Likely. Waring isn't fussy about who he uses for his experiments. And Jeff is always there with him."

"If he's so fond of Greta, why did he whip her the other night?"

Susie's lip curled. "That's part of it! Don't ask me to explain. Some of the people here are sicker than others."

"So it seems," Rose agreed. "Frank asked me to move in with him. He offered to get rid of Greta."

The tiny girl turned around to face Rose and laughed. "That's funny! She never was his girl!"

"I felt that. So you don't adivse me to accept his offer?"

"You'd have more fun jumping off the cliff. At least that would be over with in a few seconds."

"Frank claims to have information about Helen."

Susie stood up. "Frank is a confirmed liar. You can't believe anything he says!"

"I was afraid of that."

"He never tells the truth if a lie will do."

Rose went on in a troubled voice: "He claims he saw Helen and Jules here, that he talked to them both. Then he says they had a quarrel with Waring and drove away one day."

Susie stared hard at her. "Do you believe him?"

"I don't know."

"If you do, it's easy for you. You know they aren't here and won't be back. You can leave before you get in more trouble."

"Yes," Rose said thoughtfully. "It would make things easier."

"Why don't you pack your things and go? You can get away before the storm breaks."

Rose frowned. "It's not that I'm anxious to leave. I do want to—but not before I've accomplished what I came to do."

"And?"

"And I can't make myself believe that a liar like Frank has given me the true facts. I think he made up that story to stop me questioning him."

"It sounds likely," Susie agreed.

Rose sighed. "I'll have to stay. If only to someway test whether he was truthful in this or not."

"You mean you're still trapped here?"

"I'm afraid so."

Susie turned to stare out at the water again. "One way or another we're all trapped. Even the ghost! You heard that the state police were here today?"

"Yes."

"They questioned all of us."

"I was questioned as well."

Susie glanced at her again. "You know what it was all about?"

"A young man driving a car past here was attacked by a woman dressed like the ghost."

"Why not by the ghost?"

"The woman had a gun."

"Maybe a ghost can use guns."

"This ghost is supposed to be two hundred years old," Rose pointed out.

"Then she should be all the wiser."

"I doubt the motorist was attacked by a ghost. The state police likely have an idea who it was. I think Waring had one of the girls here dress like the ghost and wear a rubber mask."

"You're saying one of our girls impersonated the ghost?"

"If there is a real ghost."

"I've never doubted that," Susie said. "And you've seen her if I'm not mistaken."

"Yes," Rose said tautly, the memory of the experience hitting her with grim vividness.

"So?"

"Someone playing the ghost committed robbery."

"And nearly murder."

"That's true. It's lucky the young man wasn't fatally shot."

Susie nodded. "As I see it, and I'm sure the police agree, Waring is getting greedy. He's no longer satisfied with having a professional burglar like Cal work the island in exchange for drugs. He's now starting this girl-bandit thing."

"I think Waring is nuts."

"Without a doubt," Susie agreed. "They gave us all a rough time today. And they'll be watching the monastery closely, ready to come back the moment they have a solid clue."

It grew darker; Rose shuddered. "There's so much I don't understand here. I'm frightened almost every minute of the day and night."

Susie stood in the gathering shadows and ominous quiet. "Sometimes I think that not only is this monastery cursed, but the island as well."

"Why do you think that?"

"Do you know the history of Pirate Island?"

"No. I judge by its name it was a gathering place for pirates in the early days."

"Yes, and there are those who claim that a good share of Captain Kidd's treasure is buried on this island. Then the Quakers came, and other settlers followed. There was Indian warfare with the usual treachery on both sides. By the time of the Civil War many of the respectable shipping families on the island were sending vessels out to deal in black ivory."

"Black ivory?"

"A term," Susie explained bitterly. "It's what they called the slave trade. No matter how much they preferred to blame the South, it was often Yankee vessels from areas like this that brought the slaves over here."

"You think the slave trade also brought a curse to the island?"

"I'd say Dark Harbor was a suitable name for a town whose leaders dealt in slavery."

The weird early darkness had settled all around them now. And the beam of distant Gull Light flashed across the sky. Night birds circled in the air over the beach and uttered their eerie cries. The two girls felt isolated on the balcony of the old monastery.

"This building has also known more than its share of tragedy," Rose said softly.

"The sailors came, wrecked on the island's reefs, and brought the leprosy."

"And it spread so fast. That must have seemed like a curse at the time."

"If the monks hadn't aided the islanders, who knows what would have happened? The disease could have spread more. More people would have been maimed and died. But the monks came and built this place."

"And so we have the ghost of Leper Mary?"

"Yes," Susie murmured, her figure blurred by the advancing shadows. "If you've seen her face you've seen all the horror of leprosy." She paused. "Waring has to have some sort of disaster overtake him. It is justice that he should. He can't carry on his kind of evil without punishment."

Rose gave her a wondering look. "You feel that way and yet you stay here?"

"Where else could I go?" Susie asked. "Not back to the East Village. I was sick there and almost died alone."

"Can't you break away from this sort of life?"

"I don't want to," Susie said stubbornly. She glanced up and added, "It's starting to rain. I just felt a drop. We'd better go inside."

They went back down the stairs to the corridor and there met Tex and Dallas. "Waring is holding a ritual," the big man told her. "You're supposed to go down there with the rest of us."

"Must I?" she asked.

He nodded. "If you plan to stay on here. Otherwise he'll notice or Jeff will tell him. Then there'll be trouble."

Rose looked at them unhappily. "I'll go down, but I

won't promise to remain. Not if there's any more brutality. And that incense bothers me!"

"It's never so bad the second time," Susie told her.

She went with the others. The members of the commune descended the stairs to the underground gathering place. Again the big cavelike room was full. Rose sat on the earthen floor at the very rear, so she could escape quickly.

The torches were already burning and their flickering gave the big cave a weird kind of light. The sounds of a storm above would be dulled. Rose was seated next to Susie.

From somewhere up on the stage a sound speaker emitted a strange chanting music. Soon Phillip Waring, attired in his crimson robe, emerged from the shadows at the rear of the stage. He had a peculiar smile on his emaciated face and his eyes were unnaturally bright.

Susie whispered in Rose's ear: "Look at him! He's really stoned tonight!"

Rose nodded. Her eyes fastened on his crimson-robed figure. Now his two female assistants brought out a circular, flat stonelike platform. When they stepped back Waring went over to one of the torches and lifted it from its sconce on the wall. Then he approached the stone and touched it with the torch. Instantly a blazing circle of flame puffed up around the stone.

Then the flames vanished and a lovely girl stood in the center of the circular stone platform dressed in a skin-tight gold costume. She stepped from the stone and began to perform an intricate dance to the chanting music. Phillip Waring returned the torch to its sconce and stood on the sidelines as the girl danced.

It went on for perhaps twenty minutes; then the girl vanished amid the shadows at the rear of the stage. Phillip Waring took the central spot again. He spoke in a strange tongue that Rose felt sure no one understood. It was, to her mind, a gimmick—so that he would not have to prepare speeches and hold the attention of his audience. This way he mesmerized them with stage-effects.

A cymbal crashed and the assistants in their brief costumes wheeled out an altar on which a lightly clad young woman lay. Then Jeff appeared holding a dagger and a wide-mouthed glass container. Phillip Waring stepped behind the altar and, murmuring, made a sign over the spread-eagled girl. Then nodded to Jeff, who handed him the dagger.

Waring lifted the dagger and it glittered in the light of the flaming torches. Then he swung it downward quickly and plunged it into the body of the young woman. Rose gasped, although she was certain of a trick. Waring dared not commit a murder while the police watched the monastery so closely.

Waring took the glass container and pressed it close to the body holding it so that it was concealed from the audience. After several moments, he held up the glass container and showed it half-filled with blood!

Holding the container of blood high he murmured again. Then he handed the container to Jeff, who vanished behind the dais with it. Next he withdrew the dagger from the girl's body and, standing to one side, clapped his hands twice. The girl on the altar sat up, staring dazedly at the audience. Rose saw it was Greta, the girl who'd been whipped on that other night. She seemed to be as heavily drugged as Waring.

Applause and murmurings of approval spread throughout the room. Waring took the girl's hand as he bowed, and then led her from the dais. The girls again came out and wheeled back the altar. The audience stirred and began leaving. The ritual had taken a little over an hour.

As they reached the big central room upstairs, Rose turned to Susie and said, "Of course all his rituals are based on magic tricks. He does them so well it's too bad he didn't become a stage magician rather than being involved in this evil."

Susie laughed derisively. "Drugs are the answer. He couldn't have any regular career on the stage and take all the stuff he does. So this gives him his drugs and the power that he thrives on."

"The same girl was in the ritual again."

"Greta," Susie said with a grimace. "Did you see how drugged she was? She behaved more like an animated doll than a live person."

"I noticed."

A loud clap of thunder rolled across the high-ceilinged

room. A flash of blue lightning followed. Rose winced as she stood there.

"Your storm has arrived, Rose."

"I could do well without it."

"It may sound bad here," Susie said, "but I can't think of a place where you'd be safer."

"I'll try to tell myself that."

"I wonder what the townspeople would say if they saw that performance tonight—or the one the other night?"

"I think they'd be even more anxious to get Waring and his evil tricks off the island."

"Not to mention his followers. I'm waiting for trouble to break any day."

"I think there will be an attempt to get the monastery out of Waring's hands," Rose agreed.

"I don't know what you plan to do, but I'm going to try and sleep through this."

"It's a good idea, if you're able to," Rose agreed ruefully. She was fairly certain that she couldn't sleep peacefully with the thunder and lightning. They went upstairs to the dormitories section and said good night. Rose entered her cubicle, feeling tense and fearful. Suddenly the lights went out!

Rose groped on the table until she found the small candleholder and its single almost-burned-out candle. She struck a match to it and was grateful for even its weak glow.

Rose sat it on the windowsill. Then she paced up and down, not wanting to change for bed until the storm abated. Soon she became weary, lay down, and closed her eyes. Because of her exhausting cliff-climbing experience, she was worn out. She almost at once fell into a deep sleep.

She had no idea how long she had slept, but when she awoke it was still dark and the candle had burned almost out. The lightning and thunder seemed to have stopped, but rain fell heavily.

Fright shadowed her face. A chill of fear raced through her body as she heard a scream come from the corridor—a high-pitched feminine scream filled with terror.

Racing to the windowsill, Rose snatched up the candleholder with its small fragment of burning candle, went to the door, and opened it. The corridor was dark and she saw no one.

Then, unexpectedly, she heard footsteps running down the corridor and a second later Greta appeared, looking completely mad. She wore some sort of flimsy white material that gave her the appearance of being clad in a flowing chiffon dress. As she came abreast of Rose she halted and stared at her with her too-bright eyes.

Rose called, "Greta!"

Greta recoiled. She pointed a trembling finger at Rose and cried shrilly, "Witch! Witch!"

"Greta! I'm your friend! Come to your senses! You're running and screaming like a wild thing!"

"No!" the other girl cried, drawing further away as she spoke. Then she turned and ran down the corridor and up the stairway that led to the roof.

Rose could only conclude that in her drug-maddened state the girl planned to hurl herself from the top of the monastery. Clutching the candleholder in her hand, Rose cried out to her to stop and followed after.

Greta had climbed the stairs in record time and was out of sight. Rose followed, quickly mounting the stairs, and hurrying out through the opened door to the pouring rain of the balcony. In a second her candle was extinguished.

She moved forward in the rain and darkness, looking for the maddened Greta. A wind had blown up and rain brushed across her face. She'd almost circled the roof when she saw Greta standing on the bench next to the wall, poised to hurl herself over the side!

"Stop!" Rose cried and raced over to the girl.

As she approached, Rose tossed away the candleholder and thrust out her hands to catch Greta before she leapt to her death. Greta turned and, seeing her, uttered another wild cry. As Rose came up and grasped her, Greta struggled wildly. Rose had never encountered such insane, brutal strength and in a few minutes her back was pressed against the low stone wall. And gazing up at the triumphant face of the madwoman, Rose realized that it was she who was now in danger. Greta was trying to shove her over the edge!

Chapter Seven

Rose fought wildly as she realized her life was at stake. The rain lashed down, making the surface of the balcony slippery and treacherous. Greta fought like an infuriated animal, clawing and screaming.

There was no point in trying to cry out and reach her. In any event, Rose hadn't the strength to scream and continue the frantic struggle. With a howl of glee, Greta again shoved Rose hard against the wall and slowly began to edge her over the side.

Then Rose saw a blurred dark form behind Greta's shoulder and recognized it as the ghost Leper Mary. The phantom came close, seized Greta's throat in her hands, and the mad girl gasped and rolled her eyes. She released Rose and struggled to free herself from the choking grip of the ghost.

Rose dodged to the left and crouched in the rain, watching the awesome spectacle of the ghost and the mad girl struggling. Greta was no match for the phantom. In a moment, she slumped to the floor of the balcony and lay still. Rose started to cross to the phantom, but suddenly she was struck from behind and blacked out.

When Rose opened her eyes again, she was stretched out on the rain-drenched balcony next to the still-unconscious Greta. Her head reeled where she'd been struck. There was no sign of the phantom or of her unseen attacker. Slowly Rose struggled to her feet and looked around. The place seemed empty.

Another gust of rain hit her face. But she was now grateful for it. It cleared her thoughts. She glanced at Greta and wondered if she were still alive or if she'd died in the savage grip of the phantom. Rose knelt by the girl and tried to check her pulse.

She was sure Greta was dead, but then she felt a faint pulse. Somehow she had to get the girl downstairs and summon help. Rose partially lifted Greta from the floor of the balcony. She began to drag her toward the door that led to the stairs.

Because of Rose's own weakened state, the task was all the more difficult. Reaching the stairs, Rose dragged Greta down a step at a time until they reached the corridor. Then she left her and rushed down to the door of the room where Tex and Dallas slept. She pounded on the door and cried out Tex's name.

Finally, he called out in a sleepy voice, "What is it?"

"Come quickly! I need you!" she shouted.

A couple of seconds later the door opened and Tex appeared in his jeans, his upper body naked. His hair was a mess and his eyes half-closed.

"What's wrong?" he demanded thickly.

"Greta!" Rose said. And she quickly told him all that had happened.

"Where is she?"

"At the bottom of the balcony stairs. I'll show you."

Tex knelt down by the still-unconscious girl. He looked grim. "She's in bad shape!"

"I know it. She was crazy before everything happened."

Tex gave her a strange look. "Before the ghost choked her?"

Rose felt ill at ease. "Don't you believe me?"

"I think you must have gotten pretty mixed up. I'll have to rouse Waring if I can."

"Shouldn't she be taken to a doctor?"

"I don't know where the doctors here live," Tex said defensively. "And I don't know what luck I'd have finding one on a night like this."

"The phone?"

"Waring won't have any phones here."

"That's silly!"

"I can't help that. I'll take her down to Waring's quarters. He'll probably give me a lot of pain for getting him up at this hour."

"He has a duty to get up," Rose replied indignantly. "He's the one who got her in this condition."

"Do you think I'd dare say that? He'd toss me out of here tonight. He wouldn't even wait for the rain to stop." Tex made no reply to this. He lifted the drenched and unconscious girl in his arms and walked along the dark corridor with her. Rose accompanied him. She was anxious to find out if Waring would send Greta to a doctor or whether he'd try to minister to her himself.

They went downstairs to the big central room and then along an unfamiliar hall to a sturdy oaken door. Tex knocked on the door and waited, his burden still in his arms.

After a moment the querulous voice of Waring sounded on the other side of the door. "Who's that?"

"Tex."

"What do you want?"

"There's been trouble. I have Greta in my arms. She's in a coma. She tried to kill herself and got hurt in the struggle."

A pause ensued. Then Waring called petulantly, "Wait, just a minute!"

Tex turned to Rose. "You'd best go back. He's going to be furious and he'll take it out on all of us."

"I don't care," Rose said firmly.

As she finished speaking, the door was cautiously opened and she was shocked to see Waring standing there in a dark bathrobe and holding a gun in his hand. It was evident he didn't trust the loyalty of his commune associates.

Tex glared at him. "There's no need for the gun!"

"I can't take chances," Phillip Waring said. "Bring her in."

Tex walked ahead and Rose followed. Phillip Waring saw her and seemed surprised. He ordered Tex to put the girl on a sofa at the other side of the living room.

Waring at once knelt and examined Greta. "How long has she been like this?"

"A few minutes. No telling what might have happened if Rose hadn't followed her and stopped her from killing herself."

The emaciated face of the commune leader was shadowed with annoyance. "I'll give her a shot of something that will serve as an antidote for the drugs she's taken."

"Will it fix her up?" Tex asked.

"It should," Waring said, moving past him to the adjoining room.

Tex turned worriedly to Rose. "I told you he wasn't going to be in a good mood."

"I knew that before I came down."

"You don't care?"

"I don't think so," she said wearily. "Too much has happened to me today and tonight."

Tex eyed the girl on the sofa grimly. "If she dies, there may be some trouble explaining it to the police."

"I would think so."

Waring returned carrying a hypo with him. He went over to the girl on the divan, held her arm, carefully sought out a vein, and then expertly plunged in the needle. Then he arose and turned to them.

"She should come around in a half hour," he said.

"What if she doesn't?" Rose asked him.

Waring looked grim. "She will!"

"How can you be sure?"

"Because I've dealt with this kind of nuisance before," Waring snapped, rage crossing his face. "And what are you doing here in my apartment giving me a third degree?"

"I have an interest in her recovery."

His eyes narrowed. "Did you choke her?"

"No. The phantom did that."

Waring stared at her, shocked. "The phantom?"

"Yes. We didn't have time to tell it all to you. Greta attacked me and almost threw me over the side of the balcony. Then the phantom came and grasped her by the throat and choked her into unconsciousness."

"What about you?" Waring asked in disbelief.

"I was hit on the head by someone as I approached the phantom."

Waring's lip curled. "That's the wildest bit of feminine fancy I ever heard."

"You don't believe me?"

"No!" He turned to Tex. "Get her out of here and see she goes to her room. I've had enough annoyance for one night."

Tex nodded meekly. "Sure. What about Greta?"

"She's going to recover," Waring said, spelling every word out as if addressing a child. "Now take that other one out of here."

"You bet." And grabbing Rose's arm roughly, he said, "Come on!"

She was going to protest, but decided against it. She let Tex shove her out of the room. And not until they were out of Waring's sight did he relax and let her arm go.

Out in the central room he turned to her apologetically. "Sorry about that!"

She gave him an angry look. "You're yellow, Tex. You hurt my arm just to please him!"

"I did it to get you out of that room before there was more trouble. He's in a nasty mood tonight and Jeff could have shown up and added to our troubles."

"At least he didn't appear."

"I wonder why . . . he generally shares the apartment with Waring. Maybe he isn't at the monastery tonight."

"He was here earlier for the ritual."

"That doesn't mean he has to be here now," Tex pointed out.

"I suppose not."

Tex frowned. "I'm going back to try and get some more sleep."

"I'm not sure I'll be able to sleep," Rose murmured.

"Count yourself lucky—you could be dead right now."

"Greta tried hard enough to kill me."

Tex looked at her hard. "I know."

They went upstairs and parted at Rose's door. Rose

went inside the dark room and realized that the lights still hadn't come on again. Wearily, she lay down for a moment. Her clothes were still wet and she was beginning to feel cold. She thought about the struggle on the roof and the appearance of the phantom. Rose slept soundly and in the morning awoke to sunshine again. The storm had passed and with it all the macabre experiences of the night. She gazed up at the light bulb which hung on a single cord from the ceiling and saw that it was burning. Sometime during her sleep the lights had come on.

She felt the back of her head. There was still a slight swelling there. She sighed, dressed, and was ready to go down and forage for some breakfast when there was a knock at her door.

"Yes?"

"It's me, Dallas."

"Come in."

Dallas opened the door. "I wanted to see how you were. Tex told me about last night."

"I'm alive. What about Greta?"

"So is she. I saw her downstairs. She looked white and pretty awful, but she's up and walking around."

Rose shook her head. "I can't believe it. She must have the constitution of a mountain lion."

Dallas laughed. "What about you?"

"I'm lucky. At least most of the time."

"What was that you told Tex about a ghost rescuing you?"

Rose stared resignedly at the other girl. "I was afraid you might ask me that."

"I can't help being curious," the tall girl replied. "Tell me what happened."

"You won't believe me if I do."

"Tell me anyway."

"Greta was ready to leap from the balcony. I went after her, but I wasn't able to reason with her. She was crazy from whatever drugs she'd taken. She struggled with me and then tried to push me over the side."

Dallas listened avidly. "You couldn't get away from her?"

"No. I tried and couldn't escape. Then from behind her came the phantom. She took Greta by the throat and throttled her into unconsciousness. And when I took a step toward her someone hit me on the back of the head. When I came to she had gone."

The freckled face of Dallas showed amazement. "Do you think it was really the ghost?"

"Who else?"

"I don't know. After that robbery, Tex decided there was someone here impersonating the ghost. You could have seen whoever that is."

Rose frowned. "I don't know whether she was ghost or human, but I owe my life to her."

Dallas studied her warily. "Are you going to stay on here?"

"Why do you ask that?"

"After an experience such as last night, I don't see why you should."

"I've made only small progress in my reason for coming here." Her eyes scanned the ears of Dallas. "I see you aren't wearing the earrings any more."

The tall girl looked nervous. "No."

"Why? Because I recognized them as belonging to Helen?"

"They didn't!"

"I'm sorry, I know differently."

Dallas turned toward the door. "I'll go now. I just wanted to see if you were all right."

"You don't want to tell me the truth do you?"

Dallas flushed guiltily. "What do you mean by that?"

"You met Helen and you know something about what happened to her, but you won't tell me."

"I can't."

"Why?"

"Because you're mistaken," Dallas replied limply. "I didn't ever meet her!"

"I doubt that. If some of you would only dare to be truthful, I could leave here. Frank says she and that Jules drove off somewhere."

"Maybe he's right."

"Susie claims he's a liar."

"Susie always talks like that. You can't believe her any more than you can Frank."

Rose looked grim. "I'm beginning to wonder if I dare believe anyone."

"I'd help you if I could," Dallas replied. And she hurried out.

It had been a repetition of a scene they'd played before. Rose was convinced that Dallas had some knowledge about Helen which she was keeping back.

Rose ate breakfast and then returned to the courtyard. She found Cal seated in the sun on the front steps of the monastery watching Tex and his helper paint the hearse. The red-bearded man smoked a cigarette, which he held in a trembling hand. He glanced up at her with a thin smile.

"Ready for another day?" he asked.

"I'm not sure," Rose told him. "I find the days and nights here rather trying."

Cal chuckled. "So do most of us."

"Have you seen Greta this morning?"

"Yes. She's over there, stretched out in the sun." He nodded to a spot across the courtyard where perhaps a half-dozen girls sprawled on blankets. They wore sunglasses and bikinis.

"She had a dreadful high last night. I wonder that she doesn't kill herself."

"She will," Cal said casually.

Rose stared at him. "You say that as if it weren't important."

He shrugged. "It happens all the time. Girls like her last maybe two or three years."

"How can you be so callous?"

Cal smiled up at her. "Because I'm taking the same route in my own way. I'm entitled, as they say."

Rose sat on the step beside him. "You know you're really all a little mad, even when you're not drugged. That's the only way to explain it. Everyone here is mentally ill!"

"Aren't you afraid to stay around? It could be catching."

Rose sighed. "You may be closer to the truth than you think."

"Waring won't let you go once he gets a hold on you," Cal warned her. "In the end it's easier to stay here with him than to make a break."

"Is that how it is with you?"

"Yes."

"You could help me if you wished. So could some of the others—I only need to know where Helen is."

Cal stared at the end of his cigarette. Then he said, "Helen is just a name to me."

"I don't believe it. She wrote me from here and I've seen one of the girls here wearing her belongings. Yet only one person admits to having seen her."

"Who?"

"Frank."

Cal shook his head. "That doesn't prove anything."

"So you all agree, but I wonder."

"Pack your bags," Cal told her quietly. "Get Tex to drive you into Dark Harbor in his pretty hearse. Then take the first ferry back to the mainland and forget you were ever here."

"I'd like to."

"Then why don't you do it?"

"Not until I know where Helen is," Rose said firmly.

"By that time the ghost may get you."

"What do you know about the ghost?"

His thin face broke into a wise smile. "Just what I'm told. I hear you had a close call last night."

"News travels fast in this place. Last night the ghost saved me."

"Another time it could be the other way around."

"I still have to remain here and take my chances." Rose got up and strolled across to where Tex was working. He was painting an intricate design of orange flowers and white tulips on the back of the hearse.

She stood watching him. "The artwork is good enough, but I can't see it on the hearse."

Tex halted, the paintbrush poised in his hand, and smiled at her. "There aren't going to ever be any flowers inside this coffin on wheels, so I'm putting them on the outside."

"Dallas stopped by to see me."

"She said she would."

"I tried to get her to talk, to tell me something about Helen. She walked out on me."

The big Texan's face was grave. "We've got to think of

ourselves. We're in this a lot deeper than you. And, anyway, we don't have anything to tell."

"Did you give her those gold earrings?"

Tex looked guilty. "Why do you ask?"

"Because I think you did. And you must have gotten them from Helen or Jules."

Tex returned to his painting. His back to her, he said, "You better go to Waring or Jeff if you're looking for that kind of information."

Rose felt frustrated. "You know that won't help. They'll tell me nothing."

"Then what can you expect from us?"

"Nothing, I suppose," Rose said with a sigh. And she turned and walked away from him. She passed Greta, stretched out in the sun, but the tall girl neither moved nor gave any sign that she recognized Rose.

Rose walked to the arched entrance in the courtyard wall and outside. She went on a few steps further, then looked back and realized that just being outside the monastery walls made her feel better. The whole atmosphere of the ancient building had been tainted by Phillip Waring and his evil.

Rose strolled on across the lawn, thinking that the people of Pirate Island were right in not wanting Waring and his group in the monastery. Perhaps if they were somehow able to oust him, his disciples might rise from their apathy and get another start. But as Susie had suggested, they would likely just move on to another commune that was as bad or maybe worse.

Had that happened to Helen? Had Rose's friend been persuaded to go to the West Coast by the devious Jules Bayliss? But what interest could the supposed poet have in her when her money was gone? Rose couldn't believe that Jules really loved Helen. And he and Waring had made her withdraw all her savings and give the money to them.

The lovely blonde girl had an impulsive streak, but was not stupid. And giving everything she owned to these two rogues surely had been stupid. The only explanation would be that Helen had not been in her right senses. Somehow Jules had induced her to take drugs and kept her on them. The things she'd done had been the result of a disordered mind.

She halted and saw that she was by the main roadway leading to Dark Harbor, Monastery Road, where the robbery had occurred the other night. By now all the village must have heard about the ghost of Leper Mary. Rose could imagine the indignation the robbery had aroused. She remembered the angry faces of the state police and their promise to keep a close watch on the monastery.

Phillip Waring had gone too far if he'd set up the phantom robbery. The island had put up with the series of thefts, but armed robbery was a more serious matter. From now on the undeclared war between the islanders and Phillip Waring would be stepped up.

Rose was so lost in her thoughts that she hadn't noticed an old gray sedan moving slowly along the highway. Now it stopped abreast of her. The window on the driver's side rolled down and a weathered old face with remarkably bright eyes peered out at her. The owner of this remarkable face wore a captain's peak cap and a dark suit.

Smiling at her, he asked, "You want a ride to Dark Harbor?"

Until that moment the thought had never struck her. But Rose made an instant decision. "Yes," she said, with an answering smile. "Can you give me a lift?"

The old man chuckled. "If you'll risk my driving, I guess I can risk your company."

"Thank you." Rose hurried across the road and let herself in the ancient car.

"That door don't work just right," the old man told her. "You have to give it a good slam."

"I did."

He sighed and stepped on the clutch. "Now we'll see if we can get this stubborn craft under way."

"Have you been driving long?"

"Only about a month," he admitted as he fumbled with the gears, managed to stall the engine, and then started the procedure all over a second time.

"You'd never driven before?" she asked in wonder, for he seemed at least eighty.

His wizened face smiled broadly. "Nope," he said. "I don't expect I'd ever get a license anywhere else, but on this island. They know I can't go far or fast."

She laughed. "I think you have a lot of courage."

"I sailed my own ship around the Horn. I'm not going to let this buggy stop me."

"I'm sure you can manage—what made you decide to begin driving?"

"Got sick of sitting on my front porch and watching everyone else go by," he told her. "Wife died some time ago and I have no kin, so I'm all alone. Seemed to me I needed something to keep me on my toes."

"I see," Rose said, amused by the old man.

The captain frowned and sputtered and finally managed to get the clutch and gears working at the same time. The car jerked forward and began to move along normally.

"Knew I could win out over her," the old man said, triumph in his tone. "I drove all the way to the point and now I'm headed back home."

"Have you driven on the mainland?"

"Nope," he said. "Haven't any ambition to, either. The island is good enough for me."

"You're probably wise."

Suddenly there was a noisy interruption. From behind them came the scream of a siren and she looked back to see one of the state troopers' cars close behind them.

At the wheel the old man looked vexed. "Now, what's the trouble? I sure as shootin' ain't speedin'!"

Rose glanced back anxiously and saw the trooper signaling behind them. "I don't know what's wrong, but I'm sure he wants you to stop."

The old man groaned. "Just when I get this thing started!" He stopped the car with a jerk and the engine died.

The trooper's car also halted, the blue light on top of it still revolving, the trooper got out, and came grimly forward to them. He came up to Rose's side of the car and she rolled down the window.

He glared at her and told the captain, "Don't you know there was an armed robbery right about here the other night?"

The old man looked puzzled. "Guess I did hear something about it."

The trooper continued to frown. "I watched you pick up this girl, Captain. Do you know she's from the monastery?"

"Nope."

"For all you knew she might have had a gun and been placing it in your ribs by now and taking your wallet."

The old man at the wheel looked astonished. "You talking about this girl?"

"Yes!"

He became indignant. "Then I say you don't know what you're talking about. All she wanted was a ride into Dark Harbor and I'm glad to have the company. What do you mean jutting your pesky nose into my business?"

The trooper now turned a violent purple. His hands gripped the window sill tightly as if to settle his nerves. "Captain, I'm not even sure you should be given a driver's license in the first place. I'm not complaining about that right now. But I am trying to protect you!"

Now the captain turned purple. He fairly bounced up and down on the ancient car seat. "Why shouldn't I be driving?"

"You're getting pretty old, Captain," the trooper said sarcastically.

"So is the best Scotch whiskey!" the captain replied promptly. "What else is new?"

The trooper took a deep breath. "I don't want trouble. I'm only doing my duty. There's a bad lot of young people over there at the monastery. This girl could be dangerous to you."

"If I weren't so old as you reminded me, I might be a dang sight more dangerous to her," the captain sputtered. "I just got this car started and was cruising nicely toward Dark Harbor when you hailed me."

The trooper turned his attention to her. "What's your name?"

"Rose Smith," she said.

"Smith?" He smiled sourly. "We get a lot of kids with that name. Why are you going to town?"

"To do some shopping."

"We keep out a smart watch for shoplifters," the trooper told her. "You got any money?"

"Yes." And she took the several dollars she'd kept from her slacks pocket and showed it to him. "There."

The trooper looked disappointed. He turned to the captain again. "If you're willing to take the responsibility for driving her in, I can't stop you. But I don't think picking up hitchhikers is a good idea, especially at your age."

"What has my age to do with it?" the captain demanded. "Roll up that window and we'll get under way before he decides you'll need a license to go shopping!"

The trooper looked grim as he stepped back. "Remember I warned you, Captain. You're doing this on your own."

"Confounded idiot!" the captain sputtered and began trying to start the old car again.

The trooper returned to his car and waited on the road behind them. She felt miserable about having caused the old man so much trouble.

"He's still watching us. Maybe I'd better get out."

"Gestapo!" the old man exclaimed angrily as he fussed with the ignition, gears and clutch. "Stay where you are!"

"But I've given you a lot of trouble."

"Never mind," he said, still busy with the car.

The trooper turned his car out and flashed by them like a streak, his siren screaming and the blue light atop revolving as he drove on toward Dark Harbor.

The captain glanced at the vanishing police car with grim distaste. "Car clown!" he snapped. And then he suddenly got the ancient vehicle started again.

"He was right in warning you; there are a lot of dangerous young people at the monastery."

"You don't look dangerous to me," the old man said.

"I hope that I'm not, but I'm only one of a large group. In fact, I'm not really one of them. I'm only staying there trying to find a missing friend."

He glanced at her. "Someone missing here on the island?"

"Yes. She came here from New York and then vanished. The last I heard of her she was at the monastery."

"Too bad! I don't like the sound of it."

"I'm trying to stay here long enough to find her," Rose said. "But they deny she was ever at the monastery. I know they are lying."

"From what you say that wouldn't bother them much."

"It's pretty hopeless."

The captain had a peculiar way of sitting up very straight without resting his back against the seat. He now had a pleased smile on his tanned, wizened face. "She's moving along nice now."

"Yes." It was true the car was moving, but not more than about fifteen miles an hour.

"It's a fine little car."

"I'm sure it is."

"Bought it from a widow. She kept it in her henhouse. Didn't drive at all after her husband died. She was going to sell it for parts, but I stepped in and bought it."

"I'm sure it was a good investment."

"Took a while to get the hen feathers out," he said, chuckling. "But she's all right now. My name is Captain Zachary Miller."

"I'm glad to know you, Captain," Rose said. "I've never met a real captain before."

"Well, I'm real enough, though I'm pretty old. Not as decrepit as that whippersnapper trooper tried to make me out."

"I'm sure you're not," Rose said quickly.

"What's your name?"

"Rose Marks. I've been using Smith because I don't want the people at the monastery to know who I really am."

Captain Zachary Miller nodded. "I knew you gave that trooper a false name."

Rose blushed. "How could you tell?"

"The way you said it."

"I guess he knew, too," she said, sighing.

"Probably," he agreed. "I handled a lot of men in my time. You get to know folks pretty well. It's kind of hard to fool an old fellow like me."

"You did take a chance in picking me up."

"No."

"Why do you say that?"

"Before I stopped the car I took a good look at you," the captain said. "I knew you were all right."

"Thank you."

He gave her a side glance. "In fact, by my standards, I'd call you a pretty young thing."

"That's very nice of you."

"Are you really going shopping in Dark Harbor?"

"I hadn't planned to; I took this ride with you almost

on impulse. But now I wonder if I might be able to find out something about my missing friend in town. She must have gone in there occasionally."

He nodded his approval. "That doesn't sound like a bad idea."

"Where to start," Rose said, "is the problem. Even in a small town I can't go from door to door asking for her."

The captain seemed interested. "That's sound thinking," he said. "Was this friend of yours religious?"

"Not especially."

"I was thinking she might have gone to one of the churches . . ."

"I doubt it. I would have expected her to go to the police if she were in trouble. But she couldn't have."

"Have you asked them?"

"No."

"Maybe you should."

"They're so suspicious of me, now," Rose said worriedly.

"Idiots!" he snapped. "What about the doctor? Do you think she might have gone to see a doctor?"

Rose gave him an excited look. "That's possible!" she replied. "Perhaps I should inquire."

He smiled. "There's only one on the island. I'll take you to see him personally. He's a friend of mine. His name is Dr. Henry Taylor and he's almost as old as me."

Chapter Eight

Dr. Henry Taylor's house was in a pleasant lane, not far from the main street of Dark Harbor. It was a Cape-Cod-style bungalow with an office extension.

Captain Zachary Miller brought his ancient car to a halt before the doctor's office. "I haven't any trouble once I get her sailing."

"You drive very well," Rose told him.

"Slow but well. We're not arriving at office hours, but if the doctor is at home he'll see us."

He got slowly out of the car and insisted on helping Rose out with an air of old-world gallantry. Then he escorted her up the gravel path to the office entrance. When they went inside a buxom, white-haired nurse greeted them. She sat at a desk near the door in a waiting room.

Captain Zachary Miller doffed his cap, revealing a glistening thatch of white hair, and addressed her. "Mrs. Riddle, this young lady wants to have a chat with the doctor about a private matter."

"She's not a patient?"

"Nope. She's looking for information about a friend. Where is Henry?"

"Out on a call," Mrs. Riddle replied. "But he's coming back shortly. He's expecting a phone message from one of the Boston clinics about a patient. So he has to be here."

"Mind if we wait for him?" the captain asked.

"Not at all," the woman said smilingly. "The doctor is always glad to see you, though I must say you don't leave us much business. You're never ill."

Captain Zachary Miller looked pleased. "The salt air, Mrs. Riddle. I'm saturated with it and it's like a tonic. I was slowing down a mite, but I'm better now that I'm driving a car."

Mrs. Riddle's jolly face broadened in a smile. "Yes. I've heard about your driving."

"I just brought this young lady from the monastery end of the island."

The woman's face turned serious. "Did you hear about the robbery there? That poor young man was lucky. If the bullet had been an inch higher it would have killed him. As it was the doctor worked hard to save him."

The captain nodded. "They don't seem to have any idea who it was."

"They know," Mrs. Riddle said indignantly. "It had to be someone from the monastery. You know they have one of those hippie communes there. I hear all kinds of terrible things are going on—and to think it was once a monastery."

The captain gave Rose an amused glance. "This young lady is from there. But she's been more of a visitor than a full-time hippie."

"You live with that crowd of shiftless people?" she asked Rose in surprise.

"I'm there for a special reason," Rose said. "That's why I want to talk to the doctor."

Mrs. Riddle looked nonplussed. The phone rang and she was kept busy for a few minutes. Captain Miller led Rose over to the chairs away from the receptionist and sat down with her.

In an undertone, he said, "Henry has practiced here for forty years. He knows everyone on the island. He's just the person for you to talk to."

Rose sighed. "I hope he may know something."

"If he doesn't he may think of someone else who might," the captain suggested. "I know Henry will help you if he can."

"Waring's crowd is getting such a bad name," Rose said. "The mere fact I've been living there almost brands me as an outlaw."

Captain Miller settled back in his chair. "Don't worry about it." He took out a clay pipe, filled it with tobacco, and began to smoke.

Mrs. Riddle was now kept busy by the phone ringing almost constantly. The captain relaxed and began to relate stories of the old days on the island.

"The big years were the whaling days," Captain Miller said musingly. "The harbors were always full of ships on their way in or out. A hundred years ago Orange Street had a half mile more whaling captains' homes than any other street in the world. You wouldn't think so today, but it was the street of the aristocracy of Pirate Island. When whaling died out the street went to rack and ruin. A lot of the fine old houses were torn down. And some of them were changed so you wouldn't recognize them."

"I've heard that the early islanders were Quakers."

"True. They came here from the North Shore of the state. For a long time it was a Quaker stronghold, but now we have a mixture of all religions."

The door of the office opened and a jaunty little man bounced in. He carried a doctor's bag and was dressed smartly but conservatively. Rose guessed at once that this was the man they were waiting for.

He walked straight across to them with a smile on his face and said, "What brings you here, Captain? I know you're not ill. Don't tell me you and this young lady are planning on matrimony and you've come for your blood tests!"

Captain Miller was on his feet now. He took the joke in good part and, with a chuckle, said, "Well, now that I'm driving a car it's hard to say what it could lead to."

"My own thought exactly," Dr. Taylor said good-humoredly. It was clear that the two old men were fond of each other.

"Doctor, I want you to meet Miss Rose Marks. She's

from New York. She's living at the monastery and she has a problem."

The doctor's gray eyebrows raised. "I should think just living at the monastery these days would be problem enough."

"She's looking for a missing friend."

"I see," Dr. Taylor said. He gave Rose close scrutiny and said, "Well, I hope I may be able to help you, Miss Marks."

"Thank you," Rose said gratefully.

"Let's go into my office. I'm expecting a call and it will be easier for me to make notes in there. Also we won't be interrupted."

Captain Taylor turned to her. "Do you want me to stay?"

"If you have the time," Rose said. "I'd value any extra opinions."

The old man looked pleased. "Very well, then," he said.

Dr. Taylor led them into his large inner office. He sat at his desk, while they took chairs facing him. His aristocratic features showed interest and concern as Rose told him her problem.

When she finished, he asked, "You think this girl was on the island a month or more ago?"

"Yes."

He reached down and opened a lower drawer of his desk and brought out some record books and placed them before him. "I seem to remember a Helen."

Captain Miller gave her an encouraging glance. "I told you this might be the right place."

"I hope so."

"Now let me look back a little," the old doctor said as he riffled through the pages of his journal. "Most of my patients are islanders whom I know or tourists. This girl fitted in neither group. And she told me she was staying at the monastery. Waring and his crowd hadn't been there long enough to be an island scandal then. It's become worse since."

"I know."

The phone rang at this point and the doctor was kept busy with a long-distance call for five minutes. "Sorry," he said, "but that was an important call."

"No need to apologize," the captain said. "We're the ones who are taking up your time."

The doctor began turning the pages of the journal once more. Then he suddenly exclaimed, "Here we are—the patient's name was Helen Grant!"

"That's right!" Rose exclaimed.

The doctor frowned. "She came here one evening during office hours. She said she'd been ill and felt she ought to see a doctor."

"She was ill at the time?"

He raised his eyes and nodded solemnly. "Yes. I had no trouble recognizing what was wrong. She was getting over a bout of hepatitis. It's all too common among the hippies today."

"What happened?" Captain Miller asked.

"I gave her a lecture and some medicine." Dr. Taylor paused and sighed. "You see she'd gotten the disease from an infected needle. Her upper arm was covered with needle marks. The girl had been on drugs."

"I've been terrified of that," Rose said unhappily.

"Did you turn her over to the troopers?" the captain asked.

"No," the doctor replied, sighing. "I suppose I should have. But she gave me a story of having been sick and having to take a daily injection of something or other. I forget the exact details, but I knew it had to be a story."

"She never took drugs until she met Jules," Rose told him.

"I don't know Jules," the doctor said, "but I assume he was one of the monastery group."

"He brought her here."

The doctor nodded. "And no doubt was the one who got her on the drugs."

"I'm sure of it," Rose agreed, nodding.

He sighed. "That is why I hesitated in notifying the police about her. I felt she'd learned a lesson and had been punished enough."

Captain Miller gave him a sympathetic look. "That was good and bad; in a sense you sent her back to him."

"I thought of that," the doctor admitted. "And I hoped it wouldn't happen."

"Neither she nor Jules are at the monastery now," Rose

went on worriedly. "Hardly anyone there will talk about them. They won't help me at all."

"They keep close-mouthed to protect each other," the doctor said.

"I suppose that is the idea," Rose said. "But I'm sure Helen is in bad trouble."

"No question of that," the doctor said gravely.

"And now that they have all her money I don't know what will happen."

Captain Miller spoke up: "There seems to be the general impression that the two left the island."

"That could be. . . ." the doctor murmured.

"Did she say anything that gave you any idea of whether she planned to stay here or not?" Rose asked.

Dr. Taylor sighed. "She looked very ill. I warned her not to indulge in any activity until she was well. That would include traveling."

"What did she say to that?"

"She said she would remain at the monastery until she was well."

"Maybe she did," the captain suggested. "She would have had time to get better and then leave before this young lady arrived."

Rose shook her head in despair. "I wasted too much time thinking about what I should do instead of coming directly here and seeing her."

"You've been at the monastery long enough to know the kind of scum she was involved with," Dr. Taylor said. "These people are not your ordinary hippies, but a group of drug addicts and criminals. The thefts we've had on the island since they've come here prove that."

"And now the robbery and shooting," the Captain added.

"It's undoubtedly a bad picture," Dr. Taylor agreed. "We have a group on the island, headed by one of the town council, trying to hit on a plan to get these people out of the monastery and off the island. But it isn't easy. This Waring is cunning."

"I've found that out," Rose declared.

Captain Miller gave her an admiring glance. "I think you must be in danger there every minute."

"Well, it isn't too comfortable."

"You're one of the few friendly witnesses who knows what is going on behind those stone walls," Dr. Taylor said.

"Still I only know a little."

Dr. Taylor glanced at the captain. "Don't you think it would be a good idea for her to talk with Derek Mills while she is in town?"

The captain's face brightened. "You're right. She might be able to offer him some ideas that would help."

Rose was bewildered by the exchange between the two old men. "Derek Mills?"

"Yes," Dr. Taylor said. "He is the councilman I was speaking about. He's in charge of the committee to try and rid us of Waring."

"I don't know that I can help him," Rose protested.

"I'm sure you can," the doctor urged. "At least you can give him a picture of what is going on inside there."

The captain nodded. "So far no one has been able to do that."

"I have attended the rituals."

"There you are!" the doctor exclaimed.

Rose gave him an anxious glance. "There is some risk in my talking about it. If I go back to the monastery I could be punished by Waring for giving away the commune's secrets."

"Punished?" the captain asked incredulously.

"Yes. I saw a girl whipped until her back was covered with bloody welts."

"The scoundrels!" Captain Miller said indignantly. "Did you hear that, John?"

"All the more reason to have this Waring punished," Dr. Taylor said. "It may be that you are too late to save your friend, Helen."

Her eyes widened with fear. "Don't say that."

"It is possible."

"Yes, I know."

"So it's wise to face up to it."

Rose sighed. "Yes."

"But whether you can save her or not you'd be doing a lot for those other unfortunates under Waring's power and striking a sound blow for law and order if you help put Waring behind bars where he should be."

Captain Miller nodded. "That's true—and Derek Mills is the man to do it."

"If you think it may do some good, I'll risk it."

"I'm sure Derek will protect you," the doctor said. "I can't see him making any moves which could be traced to you until he is positive you're protected."

"Derek is no fool," the captain said.

"Very well," Rose said, won over by their talk. "I'll see him if he likes."

"I'm sure he'll be interested," the doctor replied. "His regular work is at the historical museum. May I call him there now and tell him you'd like to talk with him?"

"Yes."

The doctor at once picked up his phone and dialed a number. Rose waited nervously as he asked to speak with Derek Mills and, after a short delay, got him on the line. By the trend of the conversation she judged that Derek Mills was very interested in hearing what she had to say.

At last the doctor put down the phone and said, "He wants you to go over to the museum at once. Do you know where it is?"

"No."

The captain spoke up. "I'll drive her."

"Good," the doctor said. "I'd take you myself, Miss Marks, but I have patients waiting for me."

"It's quite all right," she said, rising.

Dr. Taylor was also on his feet. He came around to her and with a solemn look on his pleasant face, said, "I want you to look on me as a friend. Come to me any time you may need help or feel you are in danger from any source."

"Thank you," Rose said sincerely.

Captain Miller joined her in walking to the door and said, "I'm not as spry as I used to be, but anything I can do to stop that Waring abusing young people I want to do!"

"That's what we need," Dr. Taylor said, smiling in encouragement. "We all must unite. It's our one hope of getting rid of that criminal."

They left the office and got back into the car. This time the old man managed to get it started with only slight trouble. Once he got it running they headed for the museum which he said was on a hill at the other side of Dark Harbor. Rose sat rather quietly, wondering if she were making a mistake or not. Somehow Waring managed to know what went on in the town. If he or Jeff learned about her conspiring against them in this way they would have little mercy for her.

But Rose knew that Dr. Taylor had spoken the truth when he'd said that it might already be too late to save Helen. It was a painful thought, since she felt that she'd been slow in going to her friend's aid. By now Helen might be dead, or on her way to some other commune on the West Coast.

What had Cal said so casually—that girls of this type were only liable to live one or two years, maybe three at the most? It was a particularly cruel kind of murder. Murder by despots like Waring, Jeff, and Jules Bayliss who used girls like Helen to provide them with money and feed their egos.

Because of what might have happened to Helen she knew she must go ahead with what she was doing. She would tell the councilman what she knew and hope that it might help him put Waring in jail.

Captain Miller glanced at her. "You feeling all right?"

"Yes, I've just been weighing it all in my mind."

"I don't blame you for that."

"I'm sure I'm doing right."

"So am I," the old captain said. "And if he tries any of that whipping with you he'd better watch out!"

Rose gave the old man a bitter look. "The trouble is that I'm afraid you'd never hear anything about it."

He frowned. "Talk to Derek and take his advice. My own is don't go back to that place."

"I'm tempted not to. But then I won't know what is happening there."

They crossed the main street and drove up a hilly side street with a number of fine homes on it. The pleasant white houses stood out against the green of the lawns. It was one of the prettiest areas of the town. And she knew that these were the houses which Cal robbed to get drugs from Waring.

"The museum isn't far from here," the captain said.

"Good."

"I'm not going in with you this time," he went on. "I think you can make out better talking to Derek alone."

"Whatever you say."

"I don't want to interfere, but I want you to regard me as a friend. I have a little place off Main Street. Anyone will tell you where to find me."

"I'll remember."

"And maybe I'll take an occasional drive out by the monastery just to keep my eye on things."

"It might be a good idea as long as you don't put yourself in danger."

The old man at the wheel snorted. "Danger! I've harpooned whales in the South Seas in my day and been pulled through the water at the end of the harpoon. It'll take more than a petty crook like that Waring to put fear in me!"

They arrived at the museum. Rose waved to him as he drove away. Then she turned and walked to the entrance of the museum. A receptionist inside the door greeted her.

"I'd like to see Mr. Derek Mills."

The woman at the desk rose at once. "Yes. Mr. Mills expects you. Come with me."

Rose followed the woman across the main lobby of the museum. The walls were decorated with various marine paintings. She could tell that it was an excellent collection.

The woman led her up a stairway and then ushered her into a bright second-floor office. Rising from the desk was a handsome young man with brown hair whom she recognized at once.

"You!" she gasped.

The young man smiled. "Yes." He told the receptionist, "It's all right, Mrs. Seaton. I can take over from here."

"Yes, sir," the woman said quietly and exited, after giving Rose another curious glance.

"I can't tell you how grateful I am for what you did for me that day," Rose said. "And I hated myself for not asking your name."

"I felt exactly the same way. I wanted to ask your name, but when I heard you were from the monastery I veered away. Please take a chair," he said, pulling a leather-covered chair over by his desk.

"Thank you." She sat down. The office was cheery and

offered a view of the rooftops of Dark Harbor far below and the ocean beyond.

"I knew I'd made a mistake in not trying to be more friendly that day," he said. "But I felt it was a tricky situation. I've been working hard to force Waring from the monastery and I was afraid I might get you in some sort of trouble if we became better acquainted."

"And I didn't know who you were or I might have tried to explain why I was at the monastery. As it was someone saw us together."

"Oh?"

"Yes. A man named Jeff who is Waring's henchman. In many ways he's even more vicious than Waring."

Derek Mills looked worried. "That's saying something. I think Waring is a very evil man."

"I have an idea Jeff tries to outdo him, if that's possible. He made mention of seeing us and threatened to talk to Waring."

"Did he?"

"I don't know. I haven't seen Waring alone since."

"He could hardly blame you for allowing me to rescue you."

"I felt I'd be able to explain if anything were made of it."

His handsome face was shadowed. "On the other hand, if they find out about your coming here it would be more difficult."

"I realize that."

"And you're willing to take the risk."

"I feel I must," Rose replied. "Dr. Taylor gave you a brief outline of why I came to the island."

"Yes. But I'd like you to go over it again in more detail," Derek said.

"Very well." Rose began a concise but complete account of all that had led to her joining the commune and of her fruitless efforts to locate Helen.

Derek listened and then said, "Helen is very fortunate in having a friend like you."

"I'm afraid I've failed her. I came too late."

"From all indications she must have left the island with that poet."

"Perhaps. And yet whenever I talk about her to those

who must have seen her at the monastery there is something strange in the way they react. You might call it mysterious or even frightened behavior."

He nodded.

"Dallas has Helen's earrings. Where did she get them? She runs from me when I press the question. Her husband is equally silent and afraid."

"Perhaps you'll find out what is behind all this when the commune is broken up. Right now most of them are too afraid of Waring to talk."

"That's true."

"If we are able to break the wicked business up," he said with a sigh, "I need information about what is going on in there. I have a committee and I want to be able to present a picture of the goings-on behind the monastery walls to them. Out of that may come the information that will break Waring's lease on the place."

"I'll tell you all I can." She was very much impressed by Mills, even more than she had been the day he'd rescued her. His whole bearing gave her confidence that maybe something would come of the campaign against Waring and the evil he represented.

He took a sheet of paper from the side of his desk and prepared to write on it. "The only worry I have is for you."

"I must take the chance—the way things are now I'm not accomplishing anything."

He sighed, his pen poised over the page. "That unhappily seems true."

"Your full-time position is as director of the museum?"

"Yes. I enjoy it. My family is an old one on the island. All my ancestors were seafaring men who made a fortune in the whaling trade. Happily my family was able to hang onto the money and invest it wisely. This was not generally true of most. We have inherited responsibility for the local civic problems. A Mills is expected to hold office and be represented on every committee."

"It's a good thing the people have someone like you to call on," she replied, impressed.

His smile was rueful. "I often wonder, though in a case like this I haven't any doubts. The island has always been free of crime and major moral problems. I don't propose to allow Waring and his commune to change that."

"I know about the house thefts. And I think I can tell you who is responsible. He's a professional burglar who has been on drugs a long while. Waring directs his efforts."

Derek was at once interested. "Tell me about him."

"The only name I know him by is Cal," Rose began. "And that is not his real name. It's short for California where he comes from. He's not a vicious person like Waring and some of the others, but he is lost to drugs."

"The local police have felt the thefts were the work of a professional," Derek agreed. "And we guessed that whoever it was must have been sent out from the monastery by Waring."

"Then there are the rituals. I saw a girl cruelly whipped at one of them. All the main gatherings are held in a big room under the monastery and there is a mass use of drugs among those present."

"Go on," he said, writing.

"There are mock killings and other weird rituals. I think some of it based on voodoo. With drugs and hypnosis Waring exerts strong powers over most of those in the commune."

Derek glanced at her. "What sort of drugs are used? Marijuana or what?"

"The whole spectrum, even hard drugs like heroin. Cal is on heroin and I'm terrified that Jules may have started Helen on it. He used to be an addict. Perhaps he still is."

"That's bad," Derek said. "I had no idea the drug problem there was that acute."

"It is," Rose assured him. "Waring is hooked on LSD and seems to use it a great deal. I think that explains a lot of his cruel and peculiar behavior."

Derek stared at the paper on which he'd been writing. "There must be some basis for getting at him there." Glancing at her again, he said, "You're willing to go into court and swear to these things?"

"Yes."

"Anything else about the rituals I should know?"

"Members of the commune are forced to attend."

"The more I hear the more I'm convinced that Waring and his associates are monsters!"

"I was sickened by it all," she said apprehensively.

"Are they keeping the place relatively clean?"

"No. It's dirty. Little attention is paid to daily living."

Derek frowned. "And there are young children in this dreadful atmosphere?"

"A great many of them."

Derek leaned back in his chair. "I'll have an emergency meeting of the committee tonight. I think we'll try and take action through the real-estate people who gave him the lease. We'll make him answer to them for property damage. It's not the worst of his crimes, but it's the best one to convict him on."

"Do you think you'll have a chance?"

"A good one. But I may have to drag you into it."

"I know that."

"One other thing," he said. "What about the robbery and the violent attack on that young man the other night? That had to be some girl from the monastery, didn't it?"

"You're talking about the ghost?"

"Yes."

"Not even the people I've talked to at the monastery seem to be sure. They are frightened by the shooting. They think Waring has gone too far."

"I heartily agree," Derek said. "That is really what got the committee going strong."

Rose gave him a knowing glance. "You are familiar with the history and legends of the island, so you would know about Leper Mary."

He nodded. "My grandfather first told me about her when I was a little boy. She is supposed to haunt the monastery and sometimes remove her veil to show her hideous face to newcomers."

"Yes," Rose said. "Some of the commune claim to have seen her."

"Really? I never put much stock in the story. And I can't say I have any true belief in ghosts."

Rose hesitated, then, in a taut voice, said, "In this instance I have to disagree with you. I believe I have seen the ghost."

Derek was surprised. "You have?"

"Yes. She came to me the first night I was at the monastery."

"That's according to legend. You're sure it wasn't some kind of a trick?"

"I don't think so. And then I saw her briefly again."

"I hardly expected to hear anything like that," Derek admitted. "But it may be there are stranger things about the monastery than I have ever guessed."

"I'm sure it was the ghost which gave Waring the idea for his robberies."

"Go on."

"The general belief in the commune is that he has a girl wearing a nun's habit and mask impersonating the ghost. And it was she who held up that young man and shot him."

Derek frowned. "You claim there is a real ghost and a pseudo one?"

"Yes."

"Wouldn't you think it more logical to assume that Waring's heard the legend and set up a fake ghost. And that she is the only one?"

Rose considered this for a moment and then, a tiny chill shooting through her, she told him: "If I'm to be truthful I must say I believe there is a real ghost as well!"

Chapter Nine

Derek stared at her with what seemed new interest. In a quiet voice, he said slowly, "I'm impressed by what you say. If you feel as strongly as that about the ghost I'll offer you no arguments."

"I do. I can't hope to explain it. But that is how I feel."

"But we have no argument when it comes to the robbery," he went on in a different tone. "The phantom figure who held up the car and shot that young man was almost certainly an impostor sent out by Waring."

"I'm not sure, but I'd say it was a girl named Greta. Waring seems to have her completely under his domination. But it could well be someone else. The point is he's making use of the legend to perpetrate the robberies."

The handsome face of the young man behind the desk was grateful. "Well, I think we've covered almost everything. And I'm most grateful to you."

"I'm glad we've met again," Rose said sincerely.

He looked at his watch. "It's well into the noon hour. I usually have lunch at a restaurant along the shore road. Would you care to join me?"

She hesitated. "I'm not really dressed for lunch."

"You look very acceptable to me," Derek said. "It's an informal spot, anyhow. I'm sure you wouldn't feel out of place."

Rose suddenly realized that she felt hungry. "Very well, then," she said. "I'd enjoy it."

They left the office. Derek paused in the main exhibition room downstairs to show her a new display of clipper-ship models, many of them vessels owned and sailed by members of his own family. He also pointed out a series of marine paintings with different scenes of Pirate Island.

His convertible had the top down and she found riding in it much more enjoyable from her journey in the captain's ancient vehicle. They cruised through town and then out along Shore Road, which ran in an opposite direction from Monastery Road, but still was on the ocean.

Seated beside him in the roadster Rose said, "My whole experience today came about from my meeting Captain Zachary Miller. He picked me up by the monastery and drove me into town."

Derek smiled. "So you've met the captain; you know he really did command several ships of his own. He's a true deep-sea sailor."

"Yes, I could tell that. He's very interesting."

"But not the best driver in the world."

"He only began such a short time ago. He deserves credit for having the courage to attempt it at his age. . . . I told the captain my story and he suggested that I talk to Dr. Taylor."

"Well, I'm very happy about that," Derek said. "I was almost tempted to drive out to the monastery again and see if I could find you."

Rose felt a sense of gratitude at his words. She had been drawn to the handsome young man from their first meeting and he seemed to be openly declaring that he, in turn, cared for her. It seemed to her that fate had intervened in having them meet again in this way.

"I feel much better now that I've talked with you," Rose said quietly. "I was really beginning to give up hope of finding out about Helen."

"You mustn't do that. If we put enough pressure on Waring I'm positive we can learn the truth."

They drove along Shore Road until they stopped at a large sprawling restaurant. The dining room looked out over the ocean and, judging by the cars parked there, the place did a brisk noon-hour business. Derek parked the car and they went inside. They were given an excellent table by a window.

Derek ordered for them and then they began to talk on a more personal basis. "So you and Helen shared an apartment together?"

"Yes. It worked out very well. I've still kept the place, though I no longer feel sure she'll be back."

"Had Helen been engaged before this Jules Bayliss came along?"

"No. She'd dated a few fellows in the same way I did. But there had been nothing serious."

The food turned out to be excellent, a marked change from what she'd been getting at the monastery.

Rose remarked, "To top off everything the food is dreadful at the monastery."

"And he's charging you a hundred a week for a mattress, poor meals, and the dubious pleasure of being a member of his group."

"Apparently he's made a business of draining young men and women of their money in return for what he claims is the new way of living."

Derek looked bitter. "Of dying might be more accurate.

"What about you? You really don't have a young man back in New York to worry about you?"

She blushed. "I'm afraid not. I have no serious alliance at the moment."

"I find that hard to believe," he said quietly, his warm brown eyes meeting hers.

"Oh, I've had two or three fellows whom I've liked," Rose said. "But somehow I've never become engaged. One of them moved to a different part of the country and we drifted apart. Another turned out to be another sort of person from what I needed and the other boy I dated the most agreed with me that we never could make a marriage go. We were exact opposites."

"Marriage is something into which one should enter cautiously," Derek said approvingly. "At least I think so."

"I'm sure you're right. At the monastery Waring assigns girls to families and they become the wife of the male leader. I think he copied the idea from the old Mormon plan, only these unions aren't even blessed by a religious service."

Derek smiled. "How did you escape one of the commune marriages?"

"I made it clear when I entered," she said. "I'm sure they have been suspicious of me ever since."

"Probably," he said. "I think I should tell you something about myself. We've done most of our talking about you."

"Have you always lived on the island?"

"No. I went to the mainland for college at Harvard. And I worked in Boston at the Museum of Fine Arts for two years. Then I returned here."

"Somehow I see you here. I'm sure this island isn't right for everyone, but it suits you."

Derek's expression became grave. "That's true. I am happy here. But my wife hasn't adapted to the island at all."

It was the first time he'd made any reference to being married. He wore no wedding ring and Rose had assumed he was a bachelor. Now he was quite offhandedly referring to his wife.

"I wondered if you were married," Rose said.

"Her name is Joyce. We were very happy for a while. Then we lost a child through a tragic accident. She was in a nervous state, anyway, and this triggered a breakdown. I had to send her to a mainland mental hospital."

"I'm sorry," Rose murmured, genuinely touched by his story. She now realized that he had been more than usually sedate for a young man of his age. And it seemed likely that this unfortunate experience had matured him beyond his years.

"So I had a double loss at one time," he went on. "My child and my wife. I didn't ever blame my wife for the accident which took my child's life, but she somehow blamed herself."

"Did she recover?"

"Yes," he said. "I was able to bring her back. She

wasn't quite her former self, but I felt sure she was on the way to health. That we could fashion some sort of a life for us. But slowly she slipped until it became evident that she was having a second breakdown and I had to take her back to the hospital."

"Is she there now?"

"Yes, the last discussion I had with the director of the hospital was not a hopeful one. He was very frank with me and he told me he feared she might never regain her health."

Rose was amazed. "He meant that she might have to be permanently hospitalized?"

"That's what it amounted to?"

"How awful! And for you!"

"I visit her regularly. Sometimes we talk and it is like the old days, but just as often she hardly knows me."

"Have you consulted other doctors?"

"There have been a series of consultations, none offering any more hope."

"So you go on."

"I go on," he agreed. "Perhaps she may get better one day. Or it may be that she is destined to remain under care until her death."

"Has her physical health suffered?"

"That is one disturbing factor," Derek Mills said worriedly. "She has lost ground in general health. The doctors have tried to build her up, but she seems to have lost her interest in living. And the will to live can be all-important."

Rose sighed. "I find it a very sad story. She obviously could have such a wonderful life here. And yet you think the island may have had something to do with her breakdown?"

"Some people do not thrive on islands," he said. "And I ought to have made a second start somewhere on the mainland after her first breakdown. I didn't realize then that bringing her back here was the worst thing I could do."

"Surely the doctors ought to have warned you."

"I've thought of that, and yet no one made a point of it. Anyhow it's too late to worry about that now. If she does improve I'll leave Pirate Island and return to the mainland."

She eyed him sympathetically. "And that will be hard for you."

"It can't matter," he said. "I'll do what is best for her. I left my ancestral home and bought a big Victorian place on Monastery Road, hoping the change of scene would be all she needed. But it wasn't the answer."

"I hope it turns out all right."

"Thanks. I'm resigned to the worst since I've had no real encouragement from a medical standpoint. But I refuse to give up hope. So I've plunged into work to keep me occupied. And now this Waring business looks as if it might give me something to do for quite a while."

"It's wonderful of you to do so much for the island."

"Family responsibility again," Derek said with a bitter smile.

"I know."

He looked at his wristwatch and said, "I've enjoyed this time with you. I hate to see it come to an end; forgive me for burdening you with all my personal problems."

"Not at all," Rose said quietly. "I'm interested in hearing them."

"Sometimes it helps to discuss them."

"I'm sure of that."

"You've also helped me tremendously in preparing a case against Waring, but now I'm concerned about your returning to that place. Why don't you let me find you a room at one of the Dark Harbor hotels?"

"I think not. Perhaps later. I ought to risk going back for a little longer. There may be other information I can get."

"That's a good point and yet the danger for you is bound to intensify every day."

Rose smiled. "Knowing that something is being done makes it easier to bear."

"I'll want to see you again," Derek said. "Not only to let you know how the meeting goes, but also to check on your safety."

Rose knew that she very much wanted to see him again. "We could meet by the cliffs."

He smiled. "Not in the same way we first did."

"I'll promise to keep my feet on the ground."

"I'll count on that," he told her. "It ought to be in the evening. Do you think you could manage it?"

She considered. "I think it would be safer after dark. I'd have a better chance to get out of the courtyard without being noticed."

"Suppose we say around nine-thirty, then?"

"Tomorrow night?"

"Yes."

"I think I can manage that," Rose said. "If I'm not there you'll know that Waring has found some means to stop me."

His handsome face was very serious. "If you're not there, I have an idea I'll storm the monastery single-handed."

"You mustn't," she told him. "It wouldn't have to mean I was in danger. Just that I couldn't get away."

"It could mean you were in danger."

"Don't think about that."

"I'm afraid I shall," he said. "You're sure you want to go back?"

"Yes. I don't think Waring will do more than threaten me. He wants to keep me there as he knows I have more money. He'll want to get all he can from me before he does anything drastic."

Derek nodded. "That offers some cold comfort."

"I suppose I should start back."

"I'll drive you."

"I don't think that would do. They'd see your car and they know you are aligned against them."

"Well, let me take you part way, at least!"

"We can probably risk that."

"I insist."

Derek paid the bill and they left the restaurant. Instead of returning to Dark Harbor, he drove her in the direction of Monastery Road. Along the way he pointed out his house.

"That's my place."

"It must have a wonderful view of the ocean," Rose said. "And you have lots of land around it."

"There's a large garden you can't see from the road,"

he told her. "I worked in it a lot before everything started to happen."

"I hope you'll soon have time to work in it again," she told him.

He drove on until the silhouette of the monastery could be seen in the distance. The sight of the fortresslike building standing out against the blue sky gave Rose an odd, uneasy feeling. She had grave misgivings about returning, but she felt she had to. She owed it to her quest for Helen. And perhaps she could find out something more of value to the young man at her side.

Derek brought the car to a stop. "Will you walk the rest of the way?"

"Yes," she said. "It's only a short distance."

His face was shadowed with concern. "I'm worried about you. You can still change your mind and go back. It's not too late."

"I've decided," she said. "I'll see you tomorrow night."

"After nine."

"Yes. I hope you have a successful meeting."

His tone was grim as he said, "I'm certainly going to do my best to rout Waring from the island. Depend on it!"

"I'll be waiting for word."

He got out and opened the car door for her. And when she got out he gave her a sober look and then surprised her by taking her in his arms and giving her a brief kiss.

He let her go with an embarrassed look and said, "I'm sorry. Please don't misunderstand that. It's just that I've suddenly discovered that I care very much what happens to you."

She touched his hand and held it for a moment. "It's all right," she said. "And don't worry. I'll manage. Better turn and drive back at once before any of them notice you're here."

She said this partly because it was true and partly because she found the parting difficult. She felt this would make it easier. And it worked.

"All right," he said quietly. "Good luck, Rose!"

"Thanks. I'm going to start walking now."

And she did. By the time she turned around he had headed the car in the direction of Dark Harbor and was almost out of sight. Returning to the monastery was going to be difficult. Knowing that she had conspired with the enemy, she would never feel quite safe in the commune again. She had seen examples of Waring's punishment.

With a deep sigh, she turned and resumed walking toward the ancient gray structure. It was a blistering, hot afternoon and she soon felt weary and tired, but she kept on at a steady pace. It took her nearly twenty minutes to reach the arched entrance in the courtyard wall. And just inside it she saw one of the hippies, Frank, leaning against an ancient motorcycle which she had occasionally seen some of the young men at the commune driving.

He wore a broad-brimmed black hat which looked fantastic in contrast to his loudly colored suede suit. A sneer distorted his weak face.

"You must like to walk," he commented.

Why do you say that?" she asked warily. She would have preferred to ignore him, but didn't think she dared under the conditions.

"I saw you get out of that car and then walk the rest of the way."

"Someone gave me a lift," Rose said, trying hard not to show she was nervous.

"Then why did they stop halfway along the road and then go back?" the ugly-faced young man asked.

She frowned. "That was as far as they were going. How do you know so much about it?"

"I drove in on the side road," Frank said with a nasty smile. "I was in Dark Harbor. You and your boyfriend didn't see me, but I saw you."

This was all too true. She knew that the side road joined with the main one a short distance from where Derek had stopped the car. It would have been easy for Frank to have seen them without their being aware of him, especially if at the moment she'd been in Derek's arms. The thought of this made her blush.

Quickly, she said, "That wasn't my boyfriend. It was someone from town who gave me a lift partway back."

Frank rolled his eyes. "What do you know about that? Was that hugging and kissing part of the deal?"

"How dare you spy on me!" she cried.

He raised a hand to pacify her. "Don't let that upset you. I saw a lot more than you think. I followed you around town all morning. I saw you at the doctor's office and at the museum and then at the restaurant, where you had lunch with that boyfriend."

Rose was aghast. And it left no doubt that he had followed her. He knew exactly where she'd gone and the order in which she'd made the calls. What really worried her was whether he'd done the following on his own or whether Waring had ordered it.

"Why did you follow me?"

He shrugged. "I figured you were up to something. And so you were!"

"There was nothing wrong in anything I did."

Frank smiled nastily. "I guess maybe Waring is the one to decide that. From what I hear the doctor and that fellow at the museum are working with some committee to put us out of here."

"Why should I be involved in that?" She felt she must make some sort of bluff. "I went to the doctor's because I wasn't feeling well. He told me the life here was bad for my health and suggested I might get a job at the museum. And so I went there for an interview."

"And going to the restaurant was part of the interview?" he asked with sarcasm.

"I was invited and I thought going might help me get the job."

"Was that why you played that romantic scene with him when you parted?"

"Maybe," Rose said, her cheeks burning. "Girls have been known to do such things."

"Sure, baby," Frank said, a wise look on his ugly face. "I don't care how friendly you are with those guys just so long as you treat me right."

"I've always been pleasant with you!"

"Come on, honey," Frank protested languidly. "I'm talking about something more than being pleasant. I made you an offer the other day and you haven't done a thing about it."

She stood there in the heat of the courtyard, hot and tired from her long walk. Her impulse was to walk away from the creepy Frank, but she didn't dare. She wasn't sure how much he knew and whether he would pass on his information to Waring. She had to remain there and try and deal with him.

"I have to think about us. We mightn't make it together."

Frank shook his head. The ugly face under the shadow of the wide-brimmed black hat held a sinister look. "We'd do all right if you played your part. Greta has moved out on me. So the coast is clear. You can move in anytime."

"I'll see."

He took a step forward and snapped a hand around her wrist and turned it until she cried out. And placing his lips close to her ear, he warned her, "That's only a taste of what Waring would do to you if he knew! You play along with me or I'm telling him everything!"

Tears smarting her eyes, she protested, "There's nothing to tell!"

He was still holding her by the wrist. "Why not let Waring decide that?"

"I won't be threatened by you," she told him defiantly.

He chuckled again. "I give you until this time tomorrow. Either you become my number-one wife or I'm telling Waring about you and your boyfriend. And when he hears he isn't going to give you any second chances. You'll wind up like your friend Helen!"

She gasped. "What about Helen? You told me she and Jules drove off somewhere."

Frank looked triumphant. "Maybe they did and maybe they didn't!"

"Tell me!" she cried. "What happened to Helen?"

"That's something else you'll find out when you play fair with me," he said. "Remember, you've got until this time tomorrow."

"You wouldn't tell Waring!"

"I will all right," he said. "I'm taking a chance not doing it now. But it's important for me to get straight with you. You and I could make a great team!"

"Let my wrist go!"

"Sure," he said. "Just remember!"

She didn't reply, but ran on into the house, her eyes filled with tears. Some of the others in the commune were scattered along the way and seated on the steps. She paid no attention to them, though she was conscious they must have been watching she and Frank argue. They stared at her with undisguised curiosity.

She rushed into the welcome cool of the central room of the monastery and then went on upstairs to her own room. She took off her clothes and put on a robe and went down to the bathroom to shower. Tex was just emerging from the bathroom and he halted to question her.

"Where were you?" the big youth asked.

"I walked to town and back. I had a lift part of each way, but I'm dead-tired and hot!"

Tex looked gloomy. "Waring doesn't like us going in to town. Didn't he tell you that?"

"He won't mind my going. I had to call on the bank to see about withdrawing some money."

Tex looked less worried. "Maybe that would be all right. Did you tell him?"

She decided it would be better to lie about this. "I mentioned it to him. He may have forgotten, but I'm going down to talk to him about it again."

He nodded. "Yeah. You better do that!"

"I will," she promised, and then went on in and took a shower. It left her feeling refreshed and with hope. But she was still aware that she was in a dangerous spot. Frank had seen her and unless she did as he asked he was determined to tell Waring everything. She didn't trust the ugly little man and felt that even if she went to live with him he might tell Waring anyway. He would be afraid for his own skin and so ready to sell her out, no matter what she did.

She went back to her room and put on clean clothes. If only she could keep Frank from doing anything until after she met Derek. She could leave tomorrow night when Derek came to meet her. Until then she had to somehow handle the ugly little man. She found herself wishing desperately she had someone to talk to.

Perhaps this was what made her go up to the balcony. Often Susie was up there. And she was the person Rose had come to trust most in the macabre atmosphere. She felt that Susan was probably her only friend. And at that she wasn't sure to what extent she could be trusted.

When she emerged from the door leading to the rooftop, she found Susie standing there. The petite girl came over to her at once in a nervous state and said, "What was all that between you and Frank?"

Rose grimaced. "Nothing pleasant."

"I'm sure of that," Susie said, her attractive face concerned. "Something's going on here. The police were here this morning and questioned Waring again."

"Do you know what it was about?"

"Probably the robbery," the other girl said. "Anyway, since then Jeff and Waring have been downstairs. Neither have shown themselves all day. I tried to find you. Where were you?"

"In Dark Harbor."

Susie's eyebrows lifted. "You know Waring doesn't want us going in there!"

"I took a chance and had bad luck."

"Frank?"

"Yes. He was in there on that motorcycle and saw me."

"That was bad luck."

"Now he's threatening to tell Waring on me if I don't move in with him."

"He's in a rage," Susie said. "Greta has left him and is living with Waring. He wants to satisfy his pride by getting someone else and you're his only hope."

"He must hate Waring for taking Greta from him. So maybe he's only threatening me, but he won't really tell Waring what I've done."

Susie gave her a worried glance. "What have you done?"

"You really want to know? You'll be party to a guilty secret."

"I don't care—you can trust me. What did you do today?"

Rose told her everything, including Derek's taking her in his arms. "That's what Frank promises to tell Waring."

Susie looked almost ill. In a taut voice, she said, "If he should tell Waring you'll never leave here alive!"

"You think it might be that bad?"

"Yes."

Rose gave the girl a searching look. She knew that Susie had more knowledge of what had happened to Helen than she'd ever told. And she felt now was the precise moment to try and pry that information from her.

"Frank said something else that upset me. He claimed

that I might wind up like Helen. And before he told me that Helen had gone away with Jules. Today he hinted that she didn't, but no one will tell me the truth."

Susie gave her a frightened look. Then in a low voice, she said, "I think I know what happened to her."

"I've always felt you did," she said. "Please tell me."

Susie seemed to brace herself. She took a deep breath and then said, "I'm almost sure that Waring beat her to death."

"Oh, no!" Rose said with a sob.

"I'm afraid so."

"Go on!"

Susie hesitated. "Jules and another fellow came here in a car with two girls—a redhead and a blonde. I'm certain the blonde was your friend Helen."

"And?"

"Jules had been here before. He brought some drugs with him and there was big celebration down below in Waring's quarters. The four who'd come in the car stayed on. Waring kept high on LSD for days at a time and Jules went around filled with heroin."

"What about Helen?"

"She and the other girl were living with Jules and the man who'd driven here with them. They kept to themselves a lot. They were here about a month or two when there was some kind of a quarrel between Waring and Jules. I think it was about drugs."

"Or perhaps money? By that time Helen had given Waring all her money."

Susie nodded. "I know that. I saw her a few times toward the end and she was taking heroin along with Jules. She'd had a complete change of personality. She became very withdrawn."

"She stopped writing to me."

"One night, when Waring was crazy with LSD, he gave both the girls a terrible whipping downstairs. I've only heard about it secondhand. The story is that one of the girls was whipped to death and the other badly hurt. Sometime in the night Jules and the other man drove off with the injured girl."

"And what about the other girl?"

Susie showed fear in her taut voice and pale face. "I've

heard it was your friend, Helen. Jeff and a fellow who isn't here any longer buried her that night in the old cemetery. They dug up one of the old graves and buried her there. I can show you the spot."

Rose's head was spinning. "Why do you think it was Helen?"

"Because I asked the fellow who helped Jeff with the burial. He said it wasn't the redhead. So it had to be Helen."

"That's how Dallas had her earrings," Rose said despairingly. "They had stripped her of any valuables."

"They'd do that all right," Susie said grimly.

"If what you say is true, Waring is a murderer!"

"I'm sure he's killed more than one person. But I only know about this."

"He should be charged with the murder. And Derek Mills will be glad to take action against him. Can you point out the grave?"

"Yes."

"If they dig it up they should somehow be able to prove that Helen is buried there."

Susie nodded. "They ought to be able to identify her. And at least they'd know it was a body. Waring would have to account for it."

"I'll have to get away from here at once. I'll go back into Dark Harbor and tell Derek."

"You'll have to be careful. Frank was right. You'll be the next one to be murdered if they discover what you're doing."

"I expected to take risks when I came here," Rose said determinedly. "Before I leave I want you to take me down and show me where that grave is."

"You can tell when you look," Susie said nervously. "There's a higher mound than the other graves and the grass hasn't grown in as well."

"We'll go down now. I don't want to lose a minute."

They left the rooftop and went downstairs. Rose was now faced with an entirely new situation. From all that she'd heard it seemed clear that Helen had been murdered. In a sense her mission had been a failure. The only thing she could do now was see that her friend was avenged.

Once she'd had a look at the grave she would leave the

monastery and walk in the direction of Dark Harbor. With a little luck she might get a lift from a passing car. She'd find out where Derek was and try and get to him before the meeting. Once she presented him with the story of the murder he could surely summon the police and order them to go to the monastery with a proper warrant and dig up the grave.

It was a macabre business and she was terrified. But she had no choice now. She followed Susie through the central hall and out of the monastery. They walked through the courtyard and turned the corner to the cemetery. Once more she saw the rows of neat tombstones before her. She remembered that the cemetery had always had a weird fascination for her and now she thought she understood. It could have been Helen, reaching out from the spirit world and trying to speak to her.

Susie walked on ahead and then halted before one of the graves. In a hushed voice, she said, "There! That one!"

Rose went close to the mound and stared down. The mound was higher than the others and the grass had not grown over it. She stared at the grave and felt that she had come to the end of her search. Helen was buried there!

Then, from behind them, came a familiar voice, "I see you're very interested in that grave, girls."

Rose turned to look into the evil face of Phillip Waring.

Chapter Ten

Rose felt a terror more keen than any she'd known in her life. She stood transfixed as she stared at the grinning Phillip Waring. He was surely the very personification of evil. He stood there with a cruel expression of triumph on his emaciated face.

"Well, haven't you anything to say?"

Susie took a step forward. "If there's anyone to blame, it's me. I told Rose I'd show her the graves."

Great beads of perspiration stood out on Waring's forehead. His eyes contained that wild light they always had when he was high on drugs.

"You never were a good liar, Susie. You brought Rose down here to give her a thrill. You told her there was a body buried here recently."

Rose finally found her voice. Standiing by Susie and facing the leader defiantly, she asked him, "Can you deny it!"

Waring smiled mockingly. "My, we're being most melodramatic today!"

"What about Helen?" she asked.

"Helen?" he repeated.

"Yes. My girlfriend. The one I came here looking for. You whipped her until she was dead and then buried her here, didn't you?"

Susie caught her by the arm. "Rose!"

"I don't care," Rose said. "There's no use in beating about the bush any longer. We may as well come out with the truth!"

Waring clapped his hands in mock applause. "What an excellent performance!"

"Tell me the truth!" Rose demanded.

"What truths? There are so many," he said jeeringly.

"Is Helen buried there?"

Waring turned to Susie and said, "I want you to do an errand for me. And I want it done at once!"

"What?" Susie asked.

"Go get Tex and another of the boys—I don't care which one. Have them come here."

Susie hesitated. "What are you going to do?"

The face of the commune leader expressed grim humor. "Since when have I confided my plans in you?"

The tiny girl stood where she was. "I won't move until you promise me you don't mean to hurt her!"

"How touching!"

"I mean it."

"Don't worry about me," Rose told the girl.

"Now that is good advice," Waring said in his urbane way. "I promise that I shall not harm a hair on dear Rose's head. But do hurry and get those boys!"

Susie gave him a dubious look and turned to Rose. "I'll be right back. Don't do anything silly."

Waring watched the girl as she hurried off in search of Tex. "That's really remarkable. I didn't think she had that much courage."

"I think you're in for some other surprises," Rose said pluckily.

"Do you?"

"Yes."

They stood there facing one another in the dying afternoon sun. She had declared herself almost completely. She had no idea what he might do, but she was certain he was planning some sort of punishment for her. She was also convinced that Tex would be used in the punishment.

Waring continued to stand there, blocking her way. "The other night you met Derek Mills out by the cliffs."

"What makes you think so?" Rose asked defiantly.

"Jeff saw you and told me all about it."

"I didn't even know who Mills was. He saved me from falling to my death when I tried to climb up the cliff face."

"Jeff didn't have anything to say about that."

"Because he didn't know about it."

Waring stared at her. "What were you doing climbing up the cliff?"

"I was on the rocks below and got caught there by the tide."

He eyed her with new interest. "You went down through the tunnel."

"Yes."

"Most people don't know about that secret passage. Why didn't you come back the same way?"

"I was frightened. Someone or something chased me down there."

"So you didn't dare make the return trip?"

"Not through the tunnel."

"The cliff face was even more risky."

"I didn't know that when I started up it."

Waring looked at her derisively. "But you soon found it out?"

"Yes."

"Where did Mills come into it?"

"I got up three quarters of the way and could make it no further. Then he came along and heard me crying for help. He sent me down a rope and rescued me."

"Was the meeting between you two planned?"

"No," she said indignantly. "It was pure chance."

"He is my enemy."

"I can't help that."

"And today you went to town."

"How do you know?"

"I know everything that happens here," he snapped. "Did you go in town to meet Derek Mills again? Was that the purpose of your visit to Dark Harbor?"

"No. You are completely wrong. I went in to do some shopping."

"I don't believe you!"

"Why not?" She wondered if Frank had told him as he'd threatened.

"You probably went in there looking for Mills." It seemed evident that Frank hadn't talked yet and Rose felt relief.

"I went to get money," she said, hoping that this would interest him.

"Indeed?"

"Yes. You told me I could. Have you forgotten?"

He looked at her uncertainly. It was clear that he had. Now he was on dubious ground. "I can't recall having given you permission to visit Dark Harbor."

"Then you've forgotten. You told me I could go to the bank."

A greedy expression showed on the face of the leader of the commune. "The fine for going to Dark Harbor without consulting me will be a hundred dollars."

"I'll pay it."

Waring didn't reply, because at that moment Susie returned with Tex and another young man.

Waring greeted Tex with, "I want you and that other fellow to get shovels. I have some digging I want you to do."

"Okay," Tex said, a perturbed expression on his normally good-natured face. He left again and the other youth followed him.

Waring gave his attention to Susie. "I'm not a complete fool," he said impatiently. "I know why you came to the cemetery. I also know what you told this young woman."

"I didn't tell her anything," Susie protested. It was clear that she was terrified of Waring. "I only brought her out here to look at all the graves."

"Let's be frank," he said. "Rose has already told me she thinks Helen is buried there."

"I still do think so."

Waring sneered at her. "I can even tell you the story that Susie told you. She said that I whipped the two girls that came here with Jules Bayliss and one of them was so badly hurt that she died."

She stared at him. "Do you deny it?"

"Let me finish first," Waring told her. "Susie also told

you that later that night the two young men drove away again taking only one girl with them—the one who survived the whipping."

"You can't prove I said any of those things!"

"I think I can," he said. "And I'll go further in telling what you said. You told this impressionable girl that my men came down here in the middle of the night and dug a grave."

She was shocked by his calm recounting of the incident and decided he was even more callous than she'd believed. Susie was standing there, looking ill.

"Isn't that so, Susie?"

The petite girl hung her head. "Everyone says there's a body there."

"I know it," he agreed. "The rumor spread through the place like wildfire. Jeff and I were secretly amused by it all."

Rose listened in bewilderment. He certainly knew all about the whispering which had been going on behind his back. And he was leading up to something—but what?

Tex and the other youth came back armed with shovels. Tex asked Waring, "What now?"

Waring indicated the fresher of the graves. "I want you to dig that up."

Tex stared at him in surprise. "You mean it?"

"I most certainly do," Waring said, chuckling.

Tex gave him a resigned look and then told the other youth, "Let's get at it, Chuck."

Tex and Chuck advanced on the grave and began to dig. They were both large, strong young men. Rose watched, her eyes large with fear and horror. What was Waring out to do? Did he wish to compound his criminal cruelty in murdering Helen by showing Rose the remains of her friend? She felt sure she would faint at the first sign of a body buried there.

After a while, Waring broke the silence which accompanied the sounds of the shoveling. "I think most of the members of the commune became very confused about that night."

Rose turned to him. "Please don't dig any further!"

He smiled. "Are you afraid of what you're going to see?"

"Yes," she said in a panic.

He spoke to the youths doing the shoveling. "Despite this young lady's fears, I want you to continue digging."

Susie turned to him in abject appeal. "Please, I'll be ill if you keep me here."

"You were anxious enough to get here in the first place," he said. "Now you'll stay."

Susie looked as if she might collapse. The scraping of the shovels in the earth set Rose's nerves on edge. She felt each shovelful of earth moved them closer to a glimpse of horror.

Phillip Waring smiled coldly at her. "You were not here that night. But Susie was. She also should know that I had some insolence from your friend Helen and her friend. I had to teach them a lesson."

"There was no need to whip them to death," Rose said angrily.

"That night I had a ritual. I was going to whip the girls in full view of the group. It normally has a better effect that way. But on this occasion we had planned to sacrifice a sheep. There was not time for the two things. I felt the sacrifice of the sheep had more significance, so I postponed the whipping of the girls for a private session afterward."

"What difference does all that make?"

Suavely Waring said, "Jules and the other three drove off that night. I told him not to show his face here again, though I know he will. He's essentially a weak character!"

"You're saying that neither of the girls were badly whipped? That Helen and the other girl went off in the car with the two men?"

He nodded. "That's exactly what I'm saying."

She pointed to the grave where the digging still continued, "Then whose body is there?"

"I want to put an end to that rumor," he said.

It was evident that he was enjoying the bizarre moment. He moved over to where the two youths were still digging and watched them for a moment. Then he raised his hand and told them to halt. He turned to the two girls. "Well, this is the moment you've been waiting for."

Rose shook her head in anger. "You are a monster!"

"Really?" he asked coldly. "Now will you both come

closer and look down into the grave. I want you to see the remains."

Susie drew back. "No!" she protested.

Waring nodded to Tex, "Bring her over. She's really very curious by nature." He turned to Rose. "Surely, I don't have to use force with you. You have such strong opinions, especially about me. I suspect you may have picked them up in Dark Harbor."

Rose gritted her teeth and braced herself for the ordeal. Susie was shoved over to the graveside by Tex and forced to look down in it. She seemed paralyzed with shock by what she saw.

Rose walked slowly to the edge of the grave and, telling herself she would not give Waring the pleasure of seeing her collapse no matter what terrible sight met her eyes, looked down.

Her reaction was much like that of Susie's. Imbedded in the parched earth was a skeleton, plainly the remains of an animal. The skeleton was intact.

Waring laughed unpleasantly. "Surprised, aren't you? It seems everyone forgot we'd sacrificed a lamb to Satan that night. And when Jeff and his helper came here after dark to make a burial it was the lamb they buried and not either of the girls who were whipped. You see how rumors are born!"

It was such an anticlimax that Rose feared she would break the pledge she'd made to herself and become ill then and there. But once again she fought to restrain her emotions.

Looking up at Waring, she said in a low voice, "Not a very funny joke."

He looked at her derisively. "You must admit that you asked for it—both of you!"

Susie gave her a despairing glance. "I'm sorry."

Waring directed his anger at the petite girl now. "You may be sure I'll find some suitable punishment for you. I do not enjoy having rumor mongers at work here."

"Don't blame her! I'm the one!" Rose said.

The leader was annoyed. "You don't have to spell this situation out for me. I'm way ahead of you." He told Tex and the youth. "Each of you take one of them and bring them along."

Almost at once Tex seized Susie and the other youth roughly grasped Rose by the arm. Waring went ahead to the black door which led to the cellars of the monastery. The two youths followed, dragging the protesting girls with them.

Waring led the way down the stone steps and took a different corridor from the one she'd taken that day. But it was just as dark. She also noticed a strong odor of dampness in the air. They paused at one point while Waring lit a lantern and then led them on once again.

Now the corridor sloped abruptly downward. When they came to the bottom of the incline two doors with barred openings could be seen in the wall before them.

Waring's evil face looked even more devilish in the glow of the lantern. "In the days when the lepers were kept here these cells were reserved for those who went mad. I think it especially apt that you two should be locked down here until you regain your senses."

"You're making a mistake. I have friends who will know and come to my aid," Rose said protestingly.

He smiled. "The unfortunate thing is that they may never find you down here. I can promise I won't tell them. So if I'm faced with any trouble you both could easily starve here and no one would be the wiser."

He stood by with the lantern as Tex forced a sobbing Susie into one of the cells and locked it with the huge padlock hanging on the outside. The other youth forced Rose into the adjoining cell and locked it.

By the faint glow from the lantern Rose saw that the cell was small, without a window save the barred one in the door, and devoid of any furniture. Its earthen floor didn't even hold a stool.

Waring peered in at her through the bars. "I'll return to talk to you later when you are in a less belligerent mood."

"There's no need to treat us this way! We have done nothing to deserve it!"

"You accused me of murder!" Waring reminded her. "You expected to find your friend's body in that grave."

"You've done nothing to prove you're not a murderer as yet," Rose warned him.

"A murderer of a sheep," he said scoffingly. "I don't think you two are apt to be lonely. There are rats down here. And I have been told that at high tide water seeps into these cells. But I really wouldn't be certain of that."

With these parting words he left, the two youths at his side. Rose heard them make their way up the steep incline of the corridor, their voices echoing hollowly as they talked. The glow of the lantern gradually vanished and the sound of their footsteps turned to silence. She and Rose were alone in that deep underground place the monks had reserved for the mad—a place deep enough so that their wild shrieks would not disturb the others in the monastery.

Rose could hear Susie sobbing. She reached up to the bars and raised herself on her tiptoes so that she could call out. "Susie, listen to me!"

The sobbing ceased and she heard the petite girl call faintly, "Rose!"

"Don't let this break you," Rose told the other girl. "Don't give up. We're sure to have a chance if we fight this. He's counting on us giving up."

"You don't know what he's capable of," Susie said fearfully.

"I have a pretty good idea."

"We'll never get out of here alive!" Susie wailed.

"At least we have each other for company. It would be worse if we were alone."

"But separated in locked cells like this!"

"We'd still be worse off if we couldn't talk to each other."

"He'll be back. He has somthing in mind," Susie warned.

"I'm only sorry I involved you in this," Rose said apologetically.

"I did what I did willingly," Susie told her. "I really thought Helen's body was buried there."

"And he knew you did. That is why he gloated over us so. But I'm still not sure that Helen isn't dead and her body buried somewhere else."

"You can't tell with him," Susie said despairingly. "I think he is in league with the Devil."

"At least he's an apt disciple."

"I'm terrified of the dark," Susie said tremulously. "I can't see anything in here."

"Nor can I."

"Do you think there really are rats here?"

"Perhaps. But they are in other places in the monastery. That doesn't mean they'll bother us."

"I hope not. And did you hear what he said about the tide coming in here?"

"I'd think that would only be under unusual circumstances." But secretly Rose was worried. They were down very deep. The corridor had inclined sharply.

"I don't know these cellars," Susie said worriedly. "I've never been down here."

"I was down once," Rose said. "I lost my way and finally came out of a tunnel onto the rocks."

"Then the cellars are on a level with the ocean?" Susie said, a new note of fear in her voice.

"One level of them. But I'm certain we're higher." She wasn't at all certain, but she didn't want Susie to become hysterical. Time enough to deal with the flooding of the cell if it happened.

Rose leaned against the heavy wooden door, feeling terribly weary. Derek had been right; she should never have returned to the monastery. But the determination to find out about Helen had driven her on. Now she could very well die without discovering the truth.

What really worried Rose was that Waring had shown his hand so clearly. Having gone this far he could hardly let her or Susie go free again. Certainly he could not let her go. He knew she'd return to Dark Harbor and continue to work against him. This time she'd really have something to tell.

But she couldn't tell anyone anything while she was locked in this underground cell. The dampness penetrated her light outfit and she felt miserably cold. It was likely that Waring had plans for dealing with each of them separately and that could be a true moment of crisis.

Rose had a mental vision of Derek's handsome, serious face and knew she ought to have listened to him. She could only hope that he might try to come to her aid earlier than he'd planned. But she knew this was entirely unlikely.

Susie called out in a faint, frightened voice, "You are awfully quiet!"

"It's all right," Rose said reassuringly. "I'm just thinking."

"I was afraid something might have happened to you."
"No."
"I'm still puzzled about finding that animal skeleton in the grave," Susie said. "The fellow who worked with Jeff doing the burial that night swore it was one of the girls."
"Perhaps it was and later they transferred the body somewhere else and put the lamb's skeleton there. Waring knew there were rumors about a girl being buried there. That could have been his way of protecting himself."
Susie said dismally: "I don't think we'll ever find out. We will either starve or drown down here."
"Don't say such things!"
"That's what he told us."
"He was only trying to torment us more," Rose said.
There was another period of silence between them. During it, Rose attempted to review everything in her mind. She still had the feeling that some of the others at the monastery knew more about what had really happened to Helen than Susie. An example of this was Dallas. She had Helen's earrings and so she must surely know where they had come from and who had given them to her. But Dallas would not talk!
Rose paced back and forth to keep warm and this didn't help much. She hadn't realized how cold it could be deep underground. She raised herself on tiptoe to stare out through the barred opening. And she saw something that made her heart leap!
She was certain she could see someone moving with a flashlight and coming down the steep ramp toward the cells. Knowing that Susie, being too short, couldn't see out her window, Rose didn't say anything. She neither wanted to raise the unhappy girl's hopes or fears. But she could see the flashlight and its bearer drawing closer.
At last whoever it was came within a few feet of the cell door. Only then did she recognize the big Texan. He came close to the barred opening and looked in.
"You in there, Rose?" he asked in a low, anxious voice.
"Yes."
From the next cell Susie cried, "Who's there?"
"Hush up, you!" Tex growled at the girl in the other cell. "It's me, Tex, and I don't want Waring and everyone else to know I'm down here."

"I didn't know," Susie said unhappily.

"What's going to happen?" Rose asked him.

"I don't know," the big youth said dejectedly. "I didn't want to help bring you two down here, but I knew Waring would treat me the same way if I didn't go along with it."

"We know."

"You shouldn't have talked to him like you did," Tex told her. "You knew he'd be in a rage about your being in Dark Harbor."

"We were going to have trouble anyway," Rose said. "Our going down to find the grave brought it on more quickly."

"My fault!" Susie lamented from the next cell.

"Didn't he give any hint of what he might be going to do to us?"

"No. He just went on kind of crazy about how he fooled the both of you."

"He did do that," Rose said bitterly.

"And he's having a ritual tonight if that means anything," Tex said.

"It could mean we're going to be publicly whipped," Susie said, fear prominent in her tone again.

"You never know with him," Tex said.

"Is Jeff around?"

"Yeah, I saw him a little while ago. He was with Waring. They both have been in a sweat since the police came back today."

"Waring can't hold out much longer," Rose said grimly. "The trouble is that he's liable to finish us before he's finally brought to justice."

"The main reason I took a chance on coming down here is that I brought you both hot coffee."

"I can use it," Rose said gratefully.

"So can I," Susie said from the adjoining cell. "I'm nearly frozen with cold."

"I've got a covered cup for each of you," Tex said. "I'll put them in through the windows."

He did and Rose accepted hers with gratitude. She knew that the Texan had only done it because his conscience bothered him. But whatever his motives, she was glad to enjoy his bounty. The coffee helped her fight off weariness and cold.

Rose took a large drink of the hot liquid and at once felt better. She told Tex through the window. "This could make an awful lot of difference with us. Thank you."

"It's all right," Tex said nervously. "I guess I'd better get back up again. He might miss me and figure what I was up to. I had Dallas get the coffee in the kitchen and then bring it to me."

"Good luck," Rose said. "And thanks. Now if you could only find the keys we'd be able to somehow get out of here."

"I think Waring has the only key for these locks."

"Couldn't you break the lock with a crowbar?" Susie asked.

"That's right," Rose said. "They looked awfully old and rusty to me."

"And strong," Tex said uneasily. "I don't think I ever saw heavier locks."

"Maybe you'll think of something."

"I'll try," he promised vaguely. "And if he keeps you down here the night I'll be back in the morning with something for you. I won't let him starve you."

"It helps to know that," Rose said.

Tex was hurrying back up to the ground level and probably hadn't heard her. She knew that he was just as afraid of Waring as the rest and it must have taken a lot of courage on his part before he decided to risk coming to their aid. He'd gone this far perhaps he'd try to do more for them next time.

"At least we have one friend," Rose called out to Susie.

"I'm surprised," Susie admitted. "I didn't think he'd dare do anything to help us."

"He is basically quite decent," Rose said thoughtfully. "It's only too bad he became mixed up in this."

"We can't tell the time here," Susie said lamentingly. "It's always as dark as night."

"Try not to think about it," Rose said comfortingly. Susie's words had brought her unhappy thoughts about the mad lepers who at one time were supposed to have occupied these cells. She could imagine them mutilated by disease and locked in the darkness day after day, perhaps year after year, to finally die in misery. Were they also destined to die in misery?

The waiting became as tormenting as the cold and the darkness. Rose did not dare begin a conversation with Susie again. She was afraid that more talk might only unnerve the girl completely. And Rose knew she herself was already close to the breaking point.

She had believed that Waring would not harm her because he planned to get a lot more money from her. But she hadn't realized that the situation at the monastery was getting so precarious he would probably have to leave at any time. He no longer could afford to play a waiting game. He'd probably just murder her, dispose of her body as he'd disposed of Helen's, and strip her of any money and valuables.

These bleak thoughts filled her mind when she heard the voices in the corridor. She glanced out her window and saw a light approaching again. This time she was sure there were two or more people approaching.

Susie had also heard the voices and now asked her, "Who is it? Who do you see?"

"I can't make out who it is yet," she told the other girl. "We'll know soon enough."

A moment later she recognized the boisterous voices of Jeff and Waring. Knowing a ritual was scheduled, she worried that torture of herself and Susie might play a prominent part in it.

Waring had a large flashlight and he came up to the window of the cell and thrust its beam at her. She had concealed the cardboard coffee container under her blouse and had warned Susie to do the same thing, so there would be nothing for Waring to find.

"Have you cooled off some?" he asked Rose.

"Just my body," she said. "My temper is at a fever point."

"You learn slow, don't you?"

"It depends."

He gave a nasty chuckle. "You're going to lose your cellmate. We're taking Susie up for the show."

Jeff now crowded by the window, a leer on his lantern-jawed face. "Wouldn't mind having Mr. Derek Mills to come by and rescue you now, would you?"

"He managed to save my life once before."

"He's not going to be able to do it again," Phillip Waring said. And then he told Jeff: "You better get the other one out and up to the meeting room."

"Right away."

From her cell Susie called out to Rose, "I'll be all right no matter what they do. Don't worry about me! Don't be afraid alone!"

Heartened by this last-minute show of courage on Susie's part, Rose shouted back, "I'll manage. Be strong!"

"I will," Susie told her, a sob catching at her voice.

Jeff laughed harshly as he unlocked the small girl's cell and hauled her out. "You'll have lots of chances to provide a show when you get upstairs."

Rose saw him drag her friend up the incline and she asked Waring, who had remained there with her, "What's going to happen to her?"

His evil, emaciated face smiled. "She'll be the feature of the ritual tonight."

"You haven't answered me."

"Twenty lashes!"

"You can't! She's not strong enough to stand it!"

"She'll stand it. We always give them a little shot of something before and afterwards. She'll be stiff and hurting in the morning, but she'll have learned her lesson. That's the way we break them."

She stared out the barred windows at the gloating face and felt a new sense of horror. "It's more than breaking her spirit, isn't it? You need her suffering! You're as much addicted to it as Cal is to heroin! You can't exist without it!"

"It's too bad you're so unreasonable. You're an intelligent girl. I'd rather have you beside me than Greta. But you went in to Dark Harbor and you talked."

"What happens to me?"

"I have something interesting in mind."

"What?"

"I dislike being hurried," he said. "You're safe enough down here. You can wait and try to guess."

With false bravery, she said, "You don't dare harm me. You know it will only be worse for you when they finally catch up with you. And that time is not far away."

He laughed softly. "It's too bad you're going to die. You never will find out about your precious Helen."

And then he left her. There was just the darkness and the damp. Plus the visions of what must be going on in the big torchlit cave upstairs. Poor Susie, drugged and whipped before all the others. The quiet pressed in on Rose. She was all alone now. No one! She began to pace up and down steadily. After a while she heard a sound, a faint gurgling sound. It continued and soon she felt the water under her feet. Waring had made no idle threat! Sea water was filtering onto the floor of the cell!

Chapter Eleven

Rose had not really believed Waring when he'd hinted about the ocean water rising in the cells during high tide. Now there seemed no doubt that this had been a true picture of what would happen. She recalled her own adventure in the tunnel and the great breakers dashing in. She still vividly remembered being caught in the backwash of the waves and the spray.

But there was no escaping from this cell and now the tide was coming in and the floor was gradually being covered with sea water. How far would the water rise? Would it be only a discomfort or would it eventually drown her?

Even a trickle presented a threat if the water came in long enough and steadily enough. She bent down and tested it for depth. It seemed to her there must be more than an inch of the cold sea water covering the earthen floor now and it had only been coming in a short time.

The idea of drowning in the dark, narrow confines of the cell struck terror in Rose. Yet she knew screaming was no use. These cells had been specially constructed in a remote part of the monastery where screams could not be heard. There was little she could do but wait and hope!

Meanwhile the water rose slowly, the eerie sound of its gurgling a torture to her. She grasped the bars of the opening in the cell door and vainly watched for a sign of someone approaching. But there was no one! And after a little she felt the cold water rise to her ankles!

It would suit Waring well to have her drown in this horrible place. Then he could take her body and leave it on the beach and the opinion would be that she had died in an accidental drowning. There need be no suspicion directed at him. It fitted all too neatly.

Rose wondered about poor Susie and what might have happened to her. The girl's spirit was already pretty well broken. A terrible whipping such as Waring proposed to give her might shatter her completely.

Rose shivered. The damp cold of the cell had increased with the influx of the water and it had not been warm from the start. How long could she last in such a place? Was there any chance of Tex returning? She knew the good-natured youth would want to, but did he have the courage? She stared into the darkness of the empty passage and prayed that he might.

The water was now just below her knees. Rose had no idea how long she'd been alone in the dark cell. It seemed an age since Jeff had dragged Susie off and Waring had remained to give her some grim warnings. Then he had gone and she'd begun this lonely vigil.

Rose was still at the barred opening of the door and now she thought she saw someone approaching her in the darkness. Whoever it was carried no light and came forward warily. Rose strained to see who it was, but couldn't make out more than a blurred figure. At last the newcomer drew near enough for her to see. Leper Mary!

"You!" Rose cried.

The phantom unlocked the padlock which held Rose prisoner. She watched with bated breath, unable to reason it out and not trying to at that moment of crisis. The phantom gave the door a gentle shake and then furtively vanished in the shadows again.

Rose tried the door and it opened easily. The water from the cell rushed out into the corridor after her and she hastened up the ramp and crouched there a distance from the cell, debating what she should do next. Help had come from a totally unexpected source. Why should the phantom help her?

She moved on up the passage. If she were lucky she might get upstairs and perhaps even out of the courtyard without being seen. She reached the main cellar and then selected the stairway which would take her up to the central room on the ground floor. On the last flight of stairs she ascended warily, listening for some sound, but there was none. The meeting was being held in another area of the great building and if she were lucky everyone would still be there.

She reached the eerily lighted central room. Fortunately she stayed close to the door in the shadows as she sized up the situation. Her heart missed a beat as she saw that Waring had stationed two of the commune toughs to guard the arched gateway which was her only hope of escape.

She could only hope they'd weary of staying at the arch and drift away, leaving it unguarded. Then she might make a break for it. But she dare not stay out there on the steps. She thought of Tex and Dallas and felt they would help her if they could. But they were likely at the meeting.

At last Rose ventured up to her own room. It would be the last place anyone would think of looking for her. Waring might not even return to her cell and find her missing until the following day. This would give her plenty of time. With these things in mind she raced down the length of the big room and hurried up the dark stairway to her room on the upper floor.

Reaching the tiny cubicle in which she'd lived since coming to the monastery, she went inside and shut the door. She trembled with cold from the wet cell. The first thing she did was to change into warm clothes. Then she went to the window and stared down into the courtyard. The guards were still there. It looked like a hopeless situation.

She turned just in time to see the door open slowly. In spite of herself she screamed. The door came fully open and she saw the thin, scarecrow figure of Cal.

The red-bearded drug addict touched his lips as a sign for her to be quiet. She nodded as he came to join her in the dark room. After he'd closed the door he said, "I saw you as you came upstairs."

"Do you think anyone else did?"

"No!"

"I tried to escape, but they have someone guarding the arch."

Cal nodded. "Waring is getting more careful now. I heard about you and Susie."

"What about her?"

Cal grimaced. "I saw them carry her out after they whipped her on the stage. I hope she lives!"

Rose moaned. "I'll swear that Waring will pay for all he's done!"

"Before you can do anything about that you have to get out of here," Cal warned her.

"I know."

"I'm going to town. Waring has set up a house for me to rob. While I'm in there I'll somehow pass the word to Derek Mills that you need him right away."

"If only you can!" Rose exclaimed, once again feeling some slight hope.

"I'll manage," he said confidently.

She studied him as closely as she could in the darkness. "You're not afraid to betray Waring?"

Cal smiled grimly. "The game is ending for him; I can afford to desert the ship. The worst it can mean is a term in a hospital prison. It won't be a new trip for me. I've been there before."

"You're wonderful!" she said emotionally and meant it. She had always felt that Cal was on her side.

"I'd say you were wonderful yourself to get out of that cell down in the lower cellars. How did you manage it?"

"Guess."

"Tell me. I have to be on my way," he said impatiently.

"The phantom came and unlocked the cell door."

"Leper Mary?"

"Either the ghost or whoever is impersonating her. And I can't believe the impersonator would do it since she's a creature of Waring's."

"I guess you'd best thank the ghost. What are you going to do while I'm on my way to Dark Harbor?"

"Stay here, I suppose."

"Risky."

"Any place in the monastery is dangerous for me now. I wish I could contact Tex or Dallas."

"They are still at the ritual," Cal said. "I saw them there when I left."

"They'd help, but they don't know I'm free."

He considered. "I could go quietly back into the meeting and let them know."

"Wouldn't Waring or Jeff catch on?"

"Not if I'm careful."

"You're sure?" she asked worriedly.

"Yes," he said. "I know how to handle it. The main thing is that you keep hidden."

"I know."

"If anyone comes to the door here you're trapped. You have no place to hide."

"Where would be better?"

"The balcony. Up on the rooftop there is at least space and plenty of dark corners."

"All right. I'll go up there. Will you tell Tex and Dallas?"

"Yes."

"I'll leave now when you do."

Cal shook his head. "No. I'll go first. Then you come a few minutes later. It will be safer."

"All right."

"I won't be back," Cal said. "And by tomorrow I'll be in the Dark Harbor jail shivering through withdrawal."

"You'll still be better off than being a slave for Waring."

"I began to think that when I watched him whipping Susie tonight. I don't think even that scum down there would have stood for it if they hadn't all been on drugs."

"He had no reason! He likes to be cruel!"

"I know," Cal said. "I'm going. Remember. Take to the roof."

"I will," Rose promised.

He left and Rose waited for several minutes, then she went quietly out into the shadowed corridor and made her way to the stairway leading to the monastery roof. She thought of her many meetings with Susie up there and her throat constricted at the thought of how her little friend must have suffered.

And she knew that Waring wouldn't be satisfied with torture where she was concerned. Nothing less than death would do in her case. Now it all depended on Cal—whether he got to Derek in time or not.

She reached the rooftop and walked out on the balcony. She saw that there was a full, bright moon and this was not helpful when her safety depended on concealment. She quickly spotted a couple of possible hiding places.

Then she went cautiously to the stone wall and peered over into the courtyard. The archway seemed very far down and the guards were still on duty. Her every nerve was on edge as she waited for Cal to appear. It seemed to take an age for him to go downstairs and deliver the message to Tex and his wife.

A frightening new thought struck her. Suppose Cal had been playing a game with her? That all his talk about helping her had been no more than that. He might have been playing a part—and all the time he might have intended to go down and tell Waring where she was.

She crouched over the stone wall, these thoughts racing through her mind. Had his sending her to the roof been his way of trapping her. She kept her eyes fixed on the archway as her doubts mounted. And then she saw him going across the courtyard wheeling the commune motorcycle. A great surge of relief shot through her.

In a few minutes, he would be on his way to Dark Harbor. With luck he'd find Derek in a hurry and help might soon be on the way. She couldn't believe it would turn out that lucky. She watched Cal halt and talk to the two guards for a moment. Then he wheeled the vehicle out through the arch and a few minutes later she heard the sound of its motor as he drove to town.

The sound of the motorcycle faded in the distance and she moved away from the stone railing of the balcony and sought a hiding place in the shadows by the door. She waited. She knew that it would be some time before Cal got back, but she felt Tex would soon be able to get away from the ritual and join her.

Just having someone to talk to would help. And Tex might have some ideas about hiding her. She realized that in her own efforts to save her life, everything else had been forgotten. She'd almost entirely stopped thinking of Helen. Once her own safety was assured she could resume her search for Helen. She felt sure with the crackup of Waring's evil commune a lot of new information would be revealed. This might perhaps include some word of Helen's fate. She was now resigned to the fact that her friend was probably dead.

She pressed against the wall and stared up at the moon temporarily hidden by a black cloud. She thought of Cal on his way to the town and of Susie stretched out somewhere in agonizing pain. The ghost was still the major miracle of her escape, the ghost coming to her rescue! Who and why? Could it have been a resentful Greta, still hurting from the pain of the horrible beating she'd taken from Waring and wanting to revenge herself on him by frustrating his plans for having Rose die in that cell?

The idea appealed to her. She felt it could be the logical answer. Greta's act might have been triggered by witnessing the needless pain which Waring had brought Susie with his whipping. It would be bound to stir grim memories in Greta's mind. And so she might have decided to rescue Rose.

Rose was so lost in these thoughts that she did not hear the approaching footsteps on the stairway until they were very near. She at once drew back further in the shadows and hoped it might be a friend. She watched the door and when it opened the huge figure of Tex emerged. She waited for a moment to be certain he was alone and then went out to greet him.

"Tex!" she called to him in a low voice.

His back was to her and now he wheeled around quickly and came up to her. "Cal said you'd be here."

"Yes. He left for Dark Harbor just a few minutes ago."

Tex's good-natured face wore a deeply troubled look. "Things were bad down there."

"I know. Poor Susie!"

"I think Waring has really gone crazy. I have Dallas watching at the bottom of the stairs to warn us if anyone comes along."

Rose sighed. "I don't want to get you two involved."

"We are involved," Tex said. "A couple just arrived at the meeting room. One of them was someone you know."

"Who?" she asked quickly, hoping it might be Helen. Even in this moment of terror she would welcome the news that her friend was still alive.

"It wasn't Helen," he said, crushing her hopes. "It was Jules Bayliss. He drove in with some other guy I've never seen before."

"If he sees me he'll know who I am," Rose said with new concern.

Tex frowned. "I think he brought stuff with him for Waring."

"Drugs?"

"Yes."

"Likely he's a courier for him."

"They're planning to drive to a quiet cove on the other side of Dark Harbor and meet someone in a boat there," Tex went on. "Sounds like some kind of a deal. Waring may be selling stuff to others down on the Cape."

"There's nothing he wouldn't do," Rose said disgustedly.

He went over to the stone railing and glanced down in the courtyard. Then he returned to her again, a scowl on his round face. "He's still got those two guarding the archway. And they're armed! He never did that before."

"Probably because he has the shipment of drugs here. And he knows the police are watching him."

"Is Cal bringing back help?" Tex asked.

"He said so."

"You'd better hope so," Tex said grimly. "You daren't leave here and if Waring should find you're up here there's no escape."

"It's still the best place for me to hide."

"How did you get out of that cell?"

"The ghost came and unlocked the door. I think it was Greta in the ghost outfit."

Tex nodded. "I didn't see her at the ritual and she should have been there."

"I think she really hates Waring and did it to revenge herself on him."

"Assuming that she is playing the ghost."

Rose smiled wanly. "If she isn't, the real ghost must have come to me and saved me. Perhaps a hundred and fifty years ago Leper Mary was a prisoner down there herself. So her ghost wanted to do for me what no one did for her."

"I suppose I'd better get back down below."

"Yes. As long as you're not seen with me you can't be blamed for anything."

"Dallas and I want to help you," the big youth said. "If Cal can take risks for you so can we."

"I don't expect it," she said, touched by the fact that he really cared what happened to her.

"I'll come back when I can."

"All right."

"I may have to do the driving when they go to the cove," he said worriedly. "If so, Dallas will let you know."

"I'll manage. Just so long as Cal gets the word in town. They should come pretty soon. Waring won't dare to keep me here when the police come for me."

Tex gave her a warning glance. "If he finds you before they do come he could hide you away somewhere or even have you murdered and your body thrown in the ocean."

"I know."

"Maybe I can figure some way to get you out," Tex said. "It will depend on whether I take the car."

Then Tex vanished down the steps and Rose retreated even further into the shadows than before. The news that Jules Bayliss had returned to the commune filled her with a number of new thoughts and misgivings. Unless he'd left Helen somewhere behind, it suggested that she must be dead. She could only pray that the police would arrive in time to catch him. Then they should be able to make him tell what had happened to Helen.

She heard the sounds of voices in the courtyard far below and assumed that the ritual had ended. This made the danger for her greater, since the members of the group would now be wandering around. It seemed that Susie was the only one besides herself who ever visited the rooftop of the monastery often.

Trying to keep her nerves in control she concentrated on thinking of Cal and his mission. With luck he could be talking to Derek in Dark Harbor at this very moment.

Derek was holding a meeting and most likely it would be at the museum. Someone would surely direct Cal there. After that it wouldn't take Derek long to call the state police and head a rescue party to get her safely out of the monastery.

No matter which way it went Waring's reign of evil was at an end. If she should kill her before Derek and the police reached her there would still be Cal to testify against the leader of the commune. And she had no doubt that Tex and perhaps Dallas would turn against Waring and tell all they knew about the wicked happenings in the old monastery.

She suddenly heard someone on the stairs and hoped it might be Dallas. The step sounded too light for the huge Tex. She waited with a pounding heart for the door to open. The figure that appeared was not Dallas. It was a slightly built male and she at once recognized Frank! He must have learned about her escape and remembered that she often came to the balcony.

If Frank knew she'd gotten out of the cell it was also likely that Waring and everyone else knew. They would search for her. To have Frank skulking about the dark rooftop was frightening enough. But to know that the others must be looking for her as well brought her to the edge of panic.

She had no true hiding place. She could only press close to the building and trust that the darkness camouflaged her. Her eyes were wide with terror as they followed Frank in his search of the rooftop.

He was almost opposite her and she saw him go rigid. He stared straight at her and then ran over. She knew that he'd seen her and that there was no use trying to hide herself any longer. She jumped up and ran to the other side of the roof.

"You!" he cried triumphantly and raced after her.

She crouched against the stone railing, a frightened animal at bay. "Please!" she begged.

"Too good for me!" he said, thrusting his ugly face close to hers. "Now you could use a friend!"

"Don't tell Waring where I am!"

"Why not?" he sneered. "Why shouldn't I?"

She knew she had no satisfying answer for this. This was his moment of revenge and at the same time his chance to make himself strong with Phillip Waring. The leader of the commune would be very grateful!

Chapter Twelve

Frank's pent-up venom spewed out of him now as he danced before her in rage on the dark balcony. He pointed a finger at her and cried, "You tried to make a fool of me! Now we'll see who's the fool!"

She closed her eyes and moaned, "All right!" She was ready for him to call Waring. All he needed to do was shout over the railing to the guards in the courtyard.

But he apparently wanted a few more minutes of gloating. "When Waring finishes with you no one will want you!" he exulted.

She opened her eyes to Frank's hate-filled face and all at once saw a dark figure loom up behind him. It was the ghost of Leper Mary.

Rose tried to hide any reaction to what she saw. And as Frank ranted at her, Rose waited with bated breath to see what the ghost would do. She didn't have to wait more than a few seconds. The ghost leaped forward and pinned Frank by the arms, pulling him backward.

He cried out in frightened rage and a vicious struggle

ensued between the hippie and the phantom. He soon freed himself partially and the struggle became less one-sided. The two careened against the stone railing. In the melee Frank caught the veil and tore it from the ghost's face. The ghost gave a terrible, piercing shriek as her horribly ravaged face was revealed.

Rose watched in terror and revulsion. An insane rage seemed to grip the phantom. She fought and clawed with renewed energy. Frank was no longer an even match for her. He broke away once and ran almost the length of the balcony, the phantom following.

Then he jumped up on the bench to be above her in the battle. She plunged forward and grasped him around the middle and he cried out in fear and tottered backward. It happened in the matter of a second! He fell back over the edge and his phantom assailant, still clinging, fell with him. Their cries echoed in the night air as they dropped far below to a certain death.

Rose stood there swaying and ready to faint. She knew that even in death Frank had betrayed her. In no time Waring and his henchmen would be on the roof. The phantom's effort to help her had only resulted in her losing her own life. Rose no longer believed the ghost was Greta wearing a mask. That nightmare face had been real!

She had to leave the roof. It made little difference if she were captured on the way down or not. She was bound to be caught if she stayed up there. She crossed to the door and raced down the stairs. When she reached the corridor below she was met by someone. It took her a moment to recognize Dallas.

"I was going up to get you. Come with me!"

It was not a time to ask questions. Rose quickly followed Dallas. The blonde girl took her to the quarters she shared with Tex. It was a room only slightly larger than the one Rose occupied. The girl didn't say anything more to her until they were in the room with the door shut.

"I don't think they'll look for you here," she said, her ear pressed to the door.

"But if they do come here and find me you'll be hopelessly involved."

The freckled face of the girl was determined. "Tex told me to do it."

"Where is Tex?"

"Down below," Dallas said. "I was watching the stairway from the corridor and I saw Frank go up. I didn't know what to do. Then I saw the phantom. And she went up there after him!"

"She tried to save me!"

"I thought so," Dallas said, nodding.

"There was a struggle. They both plunged over the side!"

Dallas gasped. "I guessed it! I heard the screams. I knew someone was falling. I hoped it would be Frank."

"I saw her face again. It was horrible. A mass of scars! And she wore no mask!"

"No," Dallas said tautly. "She wore no mask!"

She stared at the other girl in the shadows. "You know who she was? She was no ghost!"

"No!"

"Who was it?"

Dallas hesitated. "Your friend!"

"Helen?"

"Yes."

"It couldn't be! What happened to her face?"

"Waring did it!"

Rose forgot everything else—the danger she was in, the deaths she'd just witnessed! All she could think about was Helen's beautiful heart-shaped face contrasted with the ghastly, scarred horror she'd seen a few minutes before.

"Tell me how," she requested in a weak voice.

"There was a quarrel. Jules had drained her of her money and then turned her over to Waring. She was already on heroin but not so far gone that she didn't want to get away from here. Waring wanted her for himself. She tried to escape one night when he was crazy with LSD. He caught her and used a length of chain to beat her across the face. She almost died. He had a few of us nurse her and warned us he'd treat us the same way if we didn't keep quiet about it. The others, including Susie, didn't know about it."

"Was she insane?"

"No. But by the time she recovered she was heavily addicted to heroin. Waring kept her on it all the time. She remained hidden in the cellars and only came out at night with that veil to hide her face. She took the drugs because it was her only escape."

"And she did the robbery and shooting?"

"Waring threatened to cut off her drugs if she didn't."

"Why didn't she let me know what had happened?"

"She went to you that first night, but you were so horrified at the sight of her face that she decided to remain a phantom."

Rose whispered, "All of you knew and no one would tell me!"

"We were afraid of Waring," Dallas said guiltily. "And later she let me know she didn't want you to find out."

"You should have told me!"

"I'm sorry." Then she made a quick motion to be silent and pressed her ear closer to the door. The alarm proved to be a real one. A moment later heavy footsteps sounded outside. Rose knew that the tall blonde's attempt to hide her was going to end in disaster.

From the other side of the door, Waring shouted angrily, "I know she's in there!"

Dallas made no reply. She motioned to Rose not to say anything, either. But it did no good. Suddenly there was a heavy pounding on the door and then it burst open. Dallas staggered back and Waring, Jeff, and Jules Bayliss came into the room.

Jules's thin face flashed recognition of Rose at once. He cried, "That's her! That's the one who lived with Helen!"

"Miss Smith!" Waring said, a grim note in his voice. "Tie her up! We'll take her with us!"

She tried to edge to the side and dodge from the room, but Jeff stepped forward and quickly grasped her. The lantern-jawed man had immense strength and although she struggled there wasn't a hope of her escaping.

She heard Waring tell Dallas, "We'll settle with you and Tex later."

Sobbing and struggling, she was literally carried down the stairway to the main floor. There Jules joined Jeff and bound her ankles, wrists, and placed a gag across her mouth. They took her on out to the courtyard, carried her across to the weirdly painted hearse, and opened its rear doors. Rose caught no glimpse of Tex nor did she hear his voice. She could only assume that Waring knew the dark-haired Texan had helped her and had eliminated him as a driver.

"We'll give her a ride in the hearse," Waring said mockingly.

Jeff grinned as he shoved her into the glass-walled body of the ancient hearse. "You're going to do it different," the lantern-jawed man said. "You'll ride in the hearse first and die later!"

"We'd better get going if we're going to make the cove in time!" Jules said, sounding impatient.

"We'll make it! Shut the doors and let's get going!" Waring demanded.

Rose had a brief glimpse of Jeff's ugly face as he closed the doors. Then she lay, terrorized, in the stuffy hearse as he got into the driver's seat and started the engine.

The hearse pulled out through the archway and onto the highway. As soon as it hit the highway it moved very fast. Rose was jolted roughly and slid to the left and right as the hearse rounded sharp curves.

Without warning the ancient vehicle swerved off the road and began a wild ride over rough ground. The jolting was incredible. Then Rose heard loud shouts, a blazing light cut across the side of the hearse, shots rang out. The bullets found their targets in the glass windows of the hearse and Rose screamed behind her gag as the glass splintered and shards hit her. The hearse came to a crashing halt and she lost consciousness.

When she came to, she was in the office of Dr. Henry Taylor. The old man bent over her as she lay stretched out on the cot in his examining room.

His pleasant old face was wreathed in smiles. "Well, I call that a pretty fast recovery from the dead!"

Rose sat up on her elbow. "What happened?"

"More than this island has ever seen before in one night—or is ever likely to see."

"Did they get Waring?"

"They got him good," the doctor said solemnly. "He's dead. A bullet through the head. Jules is dead, too, he ran in front of the troopers' car. The only one of the three alive is Jeff and he has a bullet through a leg. He'll live to face a jury."

"I'm glad," she said, thinking of all he had done.

"They found more than a half pound of heroin under the front seat of the hearse. That ought to take care of getting rid of your friends at the monastery."

"Cal did deliver the message then?"

Dr. Taylor chuckled. "Came straight to the council meeting."

"Where is Derek?"

"He went on to the monastery. You'll stay here for a spell until we're sure you're all right."

"I'm all right," she said with a sigh.

Rose hadn't realized yet what a toll her experiences took. Nor did she know about the awful nightmares that soon would haunt her, the guilt feelings caused by not getting to Helen sooner, and the awful memory of that ravaged face.

Rose spent almost two more months at Dark Harbor and during that period many things happened, including the deepening of her friendship with Derek Mills.

She lived first with Dr. Taylor and then moved to a boardinghouse. Most of the hippies were routed from the monastery. The ones guilty of running drugs and other offenses stood trial. The innocent ones like Tex, Dallas, and perhaps a dozen others were allowed to live on at the monastery until they could find somewhere else to go.

Susie was restored to health by Dr. Taylor and he persuaded her to return to her parents. Tex and Dallas became popular members of the staff at one of the summer hotels. And Cal had long ago been sent to Boston and a drug rehabilitation center.

Dr. Henry Taylor was not too optimistic about his chances for long-term recovery, but he said, "It's the best place available and it may straighten him out."

Rose and Derek spent many magic-filled days and nights in each other's company, until at last the ugly period at the monastery became a clouded memory. Only then did Dr. Taylor agree that she could return to New York.

The night before she left Captain Miller had her and

Derek to dinner at his place. He beamed at her happily and told her, "One of the best things which ever came out of my driving a car was meeting you."

It was a pleasant moonlit night, so they took a short drive after leaving the captain. Derek parked his car on a point overlooking the silver of the ocean.

"Must you go?"

"Yes."

"I could find you a job at the museum."

"I know."

"But you want to return to New York?"

"I must." She gave him a knowing look as they sat there in the semi-darkness of the car's front seat. "We both have our responsibilities."

"Yes, that's true," he admitted, sighing.

"It's best this way. I probably have stayed too long."

"No. I've dreaded the moment of our good-bye. I don't know how we'll handle tomorrow."

She smiled sadly. "After all we've gone through together it shouldn't be too hard."

"I don't look forward to it."

"I'll never forget the island or you," she said. "And perhaps I'll come back one day."

"Rose," he said, then hesitated. "I'm not sure I can go on without you or that I even want to."

"I know that you will," she told him. "You have your work; the island needs so many improvements. You'll keep busy."

"Can I keep busy enough?" he wondered.

She touched his hand. "I'll have the captain tell me all that happens. He's going to send me what he calls a journal regularly."

"Rose!" Derek said softly and drew her slowly to him for a long embrace. When it ended he started the car without a word and drove her home.

In the end the moment of parting had not been all that difficult. Perhaps because they both believed that they would one day be together again. Rose stood away from the ferry railing as the vessel drew in to the wharf on the mainland. In a few minutes she'd be boarding the bus for New York.

The island was behind her, but yet it would always be with her. The good memories and the bad were etched in her mind. Dark Harbor had become a part of her life and whether she wanted to admit it or not her heart remained there.